Mr *SOON* COME

Jasmine Johnson

The
X
Press

Published by
The X Press
PO Box 25694
London, N17 6FP
Tel: 020 8801 2100
Fax: 020 8885 1322
E-mail: vibes@xpress.co.uk

Printed by Bookmarque, London U.K.

Distributed in the U.K. by Turnaround Distribution
Unit 3, Olympia Trading Estate, Coburg Road, London N22 6TZ
Tel: 020 8829 3000
Fax: 020 8881 5088

Distributed in the U.S. by National Book Network
15200 NBN Way, Blue Ridge Summit, PA 17214
Tel: 717 794 3800

ISBN 1-902934-15-6

Author's ACKNOWLEDGMENTS

Respect to

my cousin Janet and sister Jacqui for lending me their ears.

Barry and Lawrence, Karen Hughes, my brother Errol.

my entire family for encouragement and support.

real friends for having faith.

(most of all) my thirteen year old son, Andre, for being patient.

To life for inspiration.

Andre, Mum, Dad, Errol, Julia, Jerome, Neil, Liz, Jacqui, Barry, Yvonne, Kevin, Auntie Dorcas, Uncle Sonny, Janet, Byron, Ikenna, Althea, Ron, Wesley, Auntie Daphne, Uncle Labon, Maryann, Phillip, Leonie, Mark, Paulette, Andrew, Jeannette, Patrick, Francis, Auntie Joyce, Uncle Prosper, Richard, Everton, Yvette, Karen, Daniel, Angie Ann & Ashley Crooks, Spicey Fingers, Foster Derby, Jeannette O'Neil

You all know why. For all sistas of endurance

Touch the life around you and tell yourself it's real
Listen to your inner self and do the things you feel. Inhale the
air about you, but exhale its foulness. Taste the sweet triumph of
your success and shout it out with loudness

Jasmine Patsy Johnson

Mr SOON COME

Birmingham, England

One poun' ten feh de wedding cake
Twenty bockles of Cola wine
All de people dem dress up inna white
Feh go eat off Johnson wedding cake
An' it's a wonder
It's a perfect wonder
While they were dancing in dah ballroom las' night.

A treasured 45 rotated on a Blue Spot. Hitting the right spot. Sonny twiddled the knobs on the radiogram, snapping his fingers and gyrating his hips. Back in Jamaica he was accustomed to gigantic speaker boxes, specially built to carry his music from one district to the other. Back then his dances were the most popular in Clarendon. Desmond Dekker, Toots and The Maytals, Prince Buster, Justin Hinds and many other stars helped his fame spread.

Nevertheless, Sonny appreciated this miniature radiogram, regardless of its inadequacies. He had bought it with his first pay packet in 'Inglann', earned from toiling in a scorching furnace in 'the black country'.

One poun' ten feh de wedding cake...

The room was as inadequate as the radiogram. But he had appreciated that too. Grateful for a roof over his head. Grateful to his Asian landlord, since the English ones would not even entertain the idea of darkies living under their roofs. And, in contrast to the scorching sun he had left behind in Jamaica, the weather was cold. He had left so many things behind. But he had brought his music.

Back home, he had been king in his arena. Women with iron-combed hair and cus-cus perfume used to come from miles around and, while hypnotised by his sounds, would offer themselves to him. Sonny would take what he was given, without any effort of asking. But he was craven. From childhood he would crave the mango that refused to fall from the top of the tree. The fruit he craved most, could not be stoned, but coaxed, nice and easy.

Gladys. Now his dear wife. Too virtuous for words.

Twenty bockles of cola wine...

The song brought back memories. Someone's wedding. Gladys had agreed to dance with him, so he set the record and left his deck unattended. She had just turned eighteen and as green as they come. This was not her first encounter with Sonny. In fact, she had had several. He was more persistent than a tiger chasing its prey. If he saw her out on street he would follow her, dishing out compliments, making her blush.

She, too, fell for his magic.

Gladys danced, awkwardly, her mama's eyes piercing through her thoughts and summoning the wrath of God upon her, and the damn right outta orderness of this tarnished man with his unbelievable presumptuousness.'

When the music had stopped, Sonny had taken her hand and led her back to her seat, closely followed by her mama's indignant gaze and the cut-eyes from women who wanted (and ones who were having) a piece of the man who had lit a raging fire inside her.

Sonny had dared to play a tune straight to mama's head:

Mammy, a love yuh daughter — no jestering
You can tell her anything you want
But I'll never let her out of my sight
Tell her how much I'm not her type
But some day she's gonna be my wife.
Mammy, a love yuh daughter
No jestering.

Mama sucked her teeth, shuffled in a silent rage, as if readying herself for the pointless battle ahead. Blasting out of oversize speaker boxes, the message was loud and clear. Sonny had thrown his corn and called a fowl. She had picked it up and it was down her belly, settling with unease.

Sonny had always known that he would marry this untainted beauty, ever since the first time he had watched her, spellbound, from the side of the river, as she bathed in the secluded spot down the steep dirt-track from her mama's yard in the Jamaican countryside.

The lengthier his pursuit of her, the more he lusted for her. But as he watched her, so her mama watched him, thinking 'Yuh cyaan hear, yuh wi' feel.'

Twenty bockles of cola wine...

As Sonny played, Gladys sat on the edge of the bed with her Bible in hand, trying to grasp the words of the Lord. She had found God and had intended to keep Him, along with her La India, (the sweet smelling pomade she used to tame her long black plaits), her cocoa butter, and her recipe for blue-drawse.

She stared at the glow of the paraffin heater, burning away in the corner of the room. Remembered the warmth she once had. Earlier, she had stared out the window at the falling snowflakes, thinking of the warm rain she had known back home, when she wore hibiscus in her hair, and picked guavas from low branches to the thud of falling mangoes and the crowing of cockerels at the break of dawn. She had longed for the friendly smiles of her people, too.

And Gladys remembered how it was in Jamaica, the first time he had danced with her. Slow. Meaningful. The first time he made love to her. Slow. Meaningful. Then the voice of her mama would echo in her head: 'Wha' sweet yuh wi' soon sour yuh.' Wha' sweet nanny goat wi' run 'im belly.'

She had always known that he would hurt her. Not physically, but emotionally, for her flesh would not stay sweet forever. For he had never been tamed.

As Sonny danced her to a new beat, as alien to her as this new country, Gladys prayed that God would nurture the child that was now growing inside her. And she hoped that it would be a son. For she feared the fate of a daughter when men like Sonny were having sons.

Gladys rocked her son to sleep. He was three years old and still a fixture to her breasts. He refused to feed from a bottle, and it was becoming unsightly.

She called him Conteh. He was the spitting image of Sonny and, shared his father's passion for music. At the age of eight he inherited music in his toes, lyrics at the tip of his tongue, gyrating hips, and what was left of the Blue Spot. With enthusiastic guidance from his father, he stripped the old radiogram, fixed it, and put it together again.

Wake up in the morning, same t'ing for breakfast.

Though Gladys feared for someone's daughter, Conteh was the apple of his mother's eyes. She prayed that he would not womanise like his father. That he would not break hearts and cause emotional pain.

The paraffin heater still burned in a corner. But the room was different now. Sonny had worked untold hours in the foundry until they had succeeded in raising the two thousand pounds they had needed to buy their first house.

Sonny changed during this time. He had found new grass to graze on. "Forbidden fruits," Gladys had called it. Women who were prepared to suffer the humiliation of being spat at in the streets for daring to taste the hungry manhood of a 'darkie'. Women who didn't give a damn, since forbidden fruits were sweeter. Now all he and Gladys shared were La India, cocoa butter, and a double bed with noisy springs. Springs that came alive once in a blue moon. And while Sonny played happily with his new-found women, Gladys consoled herself and her son by singing:

Yes, Jesus loves me
Yes, Jesus loves me
Yes, Jesus loves me
The Bible tells me so.

Sometimes, 'I hear the sound of distant drums.' Sometimes 'Wash, wash, all my troubles away.' And sometimes, 'Somewhere between your heart an' mine.' And sometimes, 'One poun' ten feh de wedding cake.' But most of all, 'Many rivers to cross.'

The years rolled by and Gladys nurtured her son and two daughters. Clinging to God like a lucky charm, she allowed Sonny the string of blondes, brunettes and redheads — *Lord, forgive him, for he knows not what he does* — for she had promised her God, one hot July day in a church in Jamaica, that she would stay, for richer, for poorer, for better, for worse, in sickness and in health.

Till death.

Gladys reflected on her youth, a far cry from the life Sonny had dished her since they left Jamaica. Hard to believe that back then she was known as 'Miss Wire-waist'.

Now she checked her velvet curtains, perfectly put together by her own hands. Touched them even though they were already perfect. Satisfied her mind, then looked around the room and hummed, 'Just a closer walk with Thee.'

She picked up her wedding photo and fixed her eyes on a young Sonny, examining his features for what seemed like forever. "Aye sah!" she sighed. It came from the pit of her stomach.

She replaced the photo, picked up her Bible and sunk it deep into her handbag. She covered her head with a church hat, pulled on her coat and headed for the front door. She was due at Sister Palmer's house within the next half hour for a prayer session. They had lots to pray about, and the Lord had better be alert.

"What a friend we 'ave in Jesus," Gladys hummed, all the way there.

ONE

The cool operator twiddled the knobs on his deck. He didn't gyrate his hips like his father before him. He was too cool.

The building vibrated. Girls gathered around. Young men slapped palms in approval. This was a boss rhythm, and the rival sound crew on the other side of the room was peeved, drowning in a sea of dub plates freshly arrived from Jamaica, rhythms raining down on them like hailstones from hell.

Me cyaan believe me eyes!

Me cyaan understan'!

Me cyaan believe seh black man really tu'n battyman.

"Me cyaan believe seh man would choose feh ride batty when there is so much pum-pum feh ride to rahtid. All who nuh ride batty put yuh hands in the air!"

The deafening sounds of whistles, 'Booyakka!' and 'Boi-boi!' echoed the crowd's agreement. The men in the audience obeyed Conteh's request, sticking their hands in the air and shouting "Rewin' Selecta!"

"Well 'ear dis!" Conteh hauled and pulled up the rhythm, teasing the ravers. When more noise convinced him of the agony he was putting out, he re-launched and came again — ruffneck style.

Conteh Gonzalez was the Don of the Birmingham dancehalls. King 'inna de ring'. From a hobby that grew from playing on a Blue Spot radiogram in his bedroom at eight years old, he most certainly had arrived. Vibes Injection sound system. It was his first love.

Second on his list of pride 'n joys was his wife Simone.

Third was his blue five series Beema, decked with the highest quality stereo system, white leather interiors and personalised number plates. This prestigious ride came out on special occasions, top off and stereo humming. Conteh had come to realise that this precious heap of metal was a serious female pulling magnet.

Fourth was a treasured heap of gold 'cargo'.

Fifth, nonetheless, was the thrill he got from screwing any female he could lay his corny lines, his hands and finally his dick on. Women who wouldn't dare lay claim to a single hair on his chest. 'It's just a one-slam,' he'd tell a few, and he'd soon put them straight if they dared to think otherwise.

Some didn't care either way. To them, having a one-slam from Mr. Vibes Injection was like eating with royalty. And sharing the sordid details with their friends afterwards would give them more rush than an E.

Mr. Vibes Injection was 'big 'bout yah'. Notorious. By numerous accounts, one of the best lovers in Birmingham.

Mista Boombastic. Mmmmmnnn… Mista Lover Lover.

The proof of the pudding was in numerous tastings.

Conteh made little song and dance about the women he bedded. Likewise, he kept his marriage low profile. Experience had taught him that.

When it came to women, Conteh had mastered the art of sophisticated bullshit via a mobile phone, during the long wait for him to knock on their doors. Practice had made him perfect, and before his victims would realise what they'd got themselves into, love, lust — or something — would cloud their minds, darken their eyes and have them chasing their own damn shadows. It would only become a problem to best friends, mothers, sisters and other associates of these women, on the outside looking in, and seeing clearly through Conteh's game.

There were even women who accepted his marriage, and in hoping that one day he might become theirs, took, without complaint, what little time he had to offer.

Simone was astute, classy, sophisticated and blessed with an abundance of innate elegance. The type of woman every bastard would like to have as his 'main' woman. The type their friends would marvel over, talk about. Fantasise over. One that would make them feel ten feet tall. The type of woman who could soften macho tear ducts by simply threatening to leave.

Simone did for Conteh what no other women had done before. He loved her in a way he couldn't explain. Before he met her, he had never really loved. When he asked her to marry him he surprised himself, let alone his idrins, who viewed marriage as the gallows. *Feh real.*

Conteh had that fatal 'oomph' Simone always looked for in a man. In the months that followed their first meeting, he would have done well to have bought shares in BT, Interflora and the perfume counter in Rachams.

The business of sound clashes, though, is a serious one. Women who become partners of sound men had to possess the patience of Job and the stamina of hunger strikers. It goes with the territory.

Simone was clearly not cut out for the bashment scene. The first time she visited one of her husband's bashments, she felt seriously out of place among bashment girls, with blue and blonde wigs, gold teeth, skintight nothings for tops, and skirts that barely covered their bumpers. She was out of place, more so since she didn't quite master the art of the 'hands-in-de-air'/'flick-up-unuh-lighter' business.

Conteh was a rough diamond and she loved him like that. Even in the days when 't'ings' were 'dread' and all his co-entertainers wore dreadlocks as a statement of blackness, he made his own unique stance by using the sacrilege afro-pick. His afro would reach remarkable heights, and at times when time would not permit him to groom it properly, he would cover it with a bandanna and secure it with a red, gold and green band.

When it came to women, Conteh reckoned he deserved gold stars. He always had 'nuff respect' from his crew, in admiration of the amount of females that lined up for his attention in the false understanding that the dick of a soundman was sweeter than any other dicks. He rarely spared a thought at times to heed one of his mother's old sayings, he'd realise that 'Every day yuh carry your bucket to the well, one day the bottom mus' drop out.'

TWO

Conteh woke from his recurring nightmare and marvelled at how real it felt. Ever since he was a small boy, he would have vivid dreams, but none so haunting as this one. Back then, Gladys called it a gift. Until a few months ago, he hadn't had a single dream for years. At least not one he could remember. But lately they seemed to be here to stay. This time it was so real, he was awoken by his own holler, a thumping heart and an ache in his left elbow.

He woke and realised that the crowbar in his dream that displayed such awkward heaviness — the one he tried so desperately to use in self-defence, was his own right arm.

Feeling sorry for himself, he sat up, stretched, mopped the sweat from his brow and tried to pull himself together. Tainted with lipstick and tinged with an unfamiliar fragrance, he kicked off the soft leather shoes that complimented his Armani suit. That fragrance ('Some cheap shit,' he thought) repulsed him now morning had broken. So too the memory of a strange woman who shared his night and whose name he would now struggle to remember. Not that it mattered to any degree. It was simply another one of his 't'ings', adding to a list so long, it was almost unbearable to think about.

He needed solace. He reached for the butt of a spliff that lay amidst the stale ashes in his ashtray. The empty Special

Brew cans lying crushed on the coffee table, were a painful reminder of how, last night, he had once again failed to drown his sorrows, and had taken the easy route to the bosom of a one night stand-in.

Jamdown, the local pirate, was his only friend. 99.6FM. It was almost as if the DJ knew where he was coming from. Tune after tune, the heart-wrenching lover's rock spoke to him loud and clearly. Dennis Brown, Gregory Isaacs, Sanchez, Janet Kay, Carroll Thompson, Louisa Marks, and many others confirmed he wasn't alone in his dilemma. People everywhere were lonely, rejected and hurting too. Men and women. Everybody's baby had left, and the plea was on for them to 'come back'. It was at times like this that Conteh realised he had a heart. For now, it was aching like hell.

Now, in the cold light of another Erdington morning, he realised that nothing could cure his pain, but the chance to hold her again — Simone, his dear wife. He knew that no matter how far he strayed, and even in the arms of ten women, he would still be lonely without her. The overwhelming need to hold her had now outweighed his pride, and he was ready to do whatever it would take to convince her that this time he would be true.

In the past, when things got rocky, Simone always broke the ice by waving the first white flag. It allowed him to maintain a front of hardness. Even though he was nearly always in the wrong, he had become accustomed to Simone's civil nature. He was waiting for that moment, but this time it seemed as if she had no intention of reconciling the matter. The longest she had stretched a silent treatment for, was six weeks. It was now three months and she was still cold towards him. Ice cold.

Right about then, Simone had already disembarked from a 767 and, in less than an hour, she would come walking through the door, but Conteh knew that it wouldn't be with open arms. She wouldn't kiss his neck and lips, and grope his balls to show how much she'd missed him. She wouldn't tell him how much she loved him, and neither would she rip his clothes off and make sweet love to him like she used to. Those days, it seemed, were gone. Conteh had messed up once too often, and now she seemed determined to take the 'midnight train' to anywhere, as long as it was away from him.

Trying to fulfil his promise of fidelity had proved an impossible task once again. There's only so much a woman can take and she swore she would leave him this time, for good.

Simone caught him out after he dared to lay it on Evadney, the sista next door. Conteh didn't know where to draw the line. To her knowledge, he had deceived her several times before

She had caught him on three previous occasions. She could not comprehend why she stayed. He had all the right words. She was under his spell.

But not this time. She had forgiven Conteh's dirty deeds too many times.

The seedy event with Evadney happened one evening when Conteh popped over to drill a few holes for her new curtain rails. When she distracted him from her walls and into her bed, he filled the need in her.

Simone was recovering from a hard day at the time. Conteh figured she was sound asleep and that he could get away with it. He was surprised on his return to see Simone waiting downstairs with a third degree look on her face. Little did he know that Evadney's moan and groaning had filtered through, waking his wife to some sensual drilling.

As if the smell of sex wasn't reeking from him, the hickey on his neck which wasn't there earlier would have likewise given the game away. She checked further, and found more clues of foul and foreplay in his briefs. Evadney didn't seem the type that would entertain even the idea of fellatio, but the smudges of lipstick (Fashion Fair's 'Playful Plum') on his Calvin Klein's revealed what an obliging bitch she was.

Conteh was cornered. He couldn't say anything so he picked up the keys to his Gulf and headed for the door, leaving Simone in a murderous mood.

He came back later that night to find his named clothes trashed! When he had got over it, he thanked God she had not ventured into the garage where his precious Beema lived. *Feh real.*

Simone wasn't the type to brawl with other women over a man, creating embarrassing scenes. She did not do the gutter stuff, so confronting Evadney at that moment was out of the question.

Simone had been watching Evadney's play for a while, and knew that her actions were the consequences of loneliness. She also knew that the only hole Evadney needed drilling was the one that was left unattended since a blonde whipped her man away from her. She only wished she would have looked farther than next door and found a man of her own. Conteh, however, was getting his meat at home and could have refused. But then, how many dogs refuse bones?

Evadney was just another member of the familiar queue of lonely black women whose men were forever looking for greener grass 'across the tracks'. Garnet, her ten-year-long boyfriend who wore dreads to express the depth of his roots, did an exodus after a blue-eyed-blonde-haired chick gave him a taste of the forbidden fruit he so often spoke about. Something turned his head, twisted his dreads, and re-directed his mind. He put his African Princess aside, flashed his locks, liberated his cock and left Evadney wondering if blondes had rum-punch flowing from the meeting of their thighs. *Feh real.*

Two weeks later Garnet was residing with Tracy in Sutton Coldfield.

Evadney could not give Garnet the son he wanted, so she spent every waking hours trying to make it up. She washed his dirty socks, briefs, cleaned years of misdirected piss from her loo seat, groomed his locks and cooked him ital food for ten years. But it couldn't have been enough, for she was left lonely, cold and rejected.

She needed some serious seeing to. In the nicest possible way. A rejected woman needs to feel wanted. But if the truth be told, she didn't figure on looking next door. After crying on Conteh's shoulders one evening when his were the only available ones to cry on, their lips touched... The inevitable was bound to happen sooner or later. She couldn't damn well help herself. This was proving too much for Simone. Unlike his other affairs, she would see Evadney daily. A constant reminder of the fact that she had her head below Conteh's navel.

This time it was D I V O R C E. Just as soon as they managed to sell the house and split the proceeds.

Guilt hastened Evadney's exit from the close. The air had become too thick for her to endure. Besides, the whole neighbourhood was 'in the know' as to why the women no longer spoke to each other. Evadney's name was mud behind their curtains, even though they all gave her plastic smiles. Her back wasn't broad enough to take the shame, so she put her house up for sale and moved back to her parents in Moseley.

What else could she have done?

The sound of rattling keys prompted Conteh to reach for the butt of another spliff. He needed one more toke to give him the courage to grovel. The courage to hold her, to tell her yet again how much he loved her, to swallow his pride and beg her to change her mind. More than ever, he wanted her to second his emotion and give him yet another chance.

He would cry if he had to. Of course black men cry too. They are made with hearts and emotions just like the women they hurt. Conteh would bawl his eyes out if he had to. He would claim it wasn't his fault, that he was addicted to sex. He would say he couldn't control his lechery even when he tried, yet his love for Simone was beyond explanation.

The sensual aroma of Paloma Picasso filled the room

and a faint 'Hi' (more like a grunt) reached his ears.

"Hi Babes." Conteh lit up and dragged vengefully on his herbal rescue. But before he could attempt another word Simone was already negotiating the stairs. It had been a hard night of false smiles, tired feet, trolleys and duty frees, and what with the heavies of her personal life, just then a refreshing shower was all she needed.

The ringing of his mobile phone interrupted Conteh's thoughts. It was Marcia, a sexy thirty-six year old who lived alone in a luxury apartment in Solihull.

Marcia didn't do much on the work front. She didn't need to. She dressed well, ate well and travelled often. They were all affordable vices to her. As were her weekly visits to a swanky health farm. She had inherited a healthy bank balance by using her brains and good looks to persuade Fred, a wealthy old white man to make her the sole beneficiary of his will. The kinky old man had a thing for black women, and when Marcia agreed to spend what he called precious moments with him, he figured that was enough to keep an old fool happy. And there's no fool like an old fool.

Fred held memories of young African women with firm asses and breasts like plums. He could almost feel the African sun beating down on his tanned body as he reminisced on the years he spent there. He was a real eccentric, and now that he couldn't get it up without the aid of Viagra, sitting nude with him in his luxury apartment whenever he wanted, didn't seem such an arduous task for Marcia. Especially after she realised what was in it for her. Fred had no close living relatives. Not that he knew of anyway. And he was rolling in it.

Having sex with a seventy-five-year-old white-man-with-balls-like-deflated-balloons-and-a-body-like-dried-up-prunes, wasn't Marcia's idea of a good time. She had been through the mill and back with bastard black men and had now decided that she had no intention of being anybody's fool again. She had drawn her own conclusion that men were only good for one thing — a dick thing. And who better to get this thing from but a married man. As she saw it, this way there would be no ties, no fancy promises and no commitment. She had decided too that she wouldn't be anybody's skivvy and as it went, she didn't need to be. She also didn't need anyone under her feet either. She wanted her freedom to come and go as she pleased. She would ask for no rose gardens, and expected none. She had been there with the slaps and the verbal abuse. The 'laying awake all night waiting for the sound of rattling keys' shit. She was definitely not going there again. Only, she had needs. Sexual needs. 'Therapy' was what she called it, and she would not deny herself that. No way.

Marcia had entered into the relationship with Conteh with her eyes open and her heart closed. She had explained at the outset, how she wanted things. Conteh had agreed.

"There are some good ones out there," her mother had said one day.

"Yeah, right. Tall, dark, handsome, wicked in bed, non-male chauvinistic and faithful, mum? I don't think so?" was her reply. Her mother's definition of 'good' was 'wimp'. Men who would stifle you, cry when you're late home from work, listen on second extensions as you chatted with your mates, run your bath even when you've just had one. Men who would throw pills down their necks when you finally found the words to say, 'I'm checking out.' Men women think they want, but when they get them, they would crave for the touch of another bastard. There had to be something in the saying: 'Women prefer bastards.'

For Marcia, wimps and bastards were out. That left one dilemma. The rest of mankind seemed to be gay, too young, too old or (more than likely) already taken, and the takers were holding on to them. Tight.

She found vibrators too much of a turn-off. Marcia wanted jam on it too, and had no reservations about it being somebody else's jam. Felt she deserved someone who could give her an orgasm — multiple ones wouldn't be sneezed at — someone who turned her on, knew how to ring her bell and had no hang ups about that good old cunnilingus. By far, the latter was the most important. She was definitely a modern gal who believed in living. So listening to shit about oral sex being nasty, and to DJs who condemned lovers who dared to eat below the navel, pissed her off to the max. She had no time for all that 'Men are from Mars, Women are from Venus' crap, either. She was no longer interested in the minds of her men; why they are the way they are, why they withdraw into the caves of their minds and all that. She had 'been there', 'tried that', and it didn't work. The only way to communicate with men, she had decided, was through sex.

She seriously had no time for the ones who held out on her pleasure zone. Men whose mental block on the oral front took as much demolishing as the Berlin Wall. Even when they know that a woman's idea of 'wicked in bed' meant a bit more than climb on, in out, in out, breathe like a panther, come, roll over, sleep. Men who will not take the time to understand that a woman's libido is not a buzz that lies somewhere between bookie shops and dancehalls, but a psychic impulse that lies somewhere between the meeting of her thighs. Men who need to be told that the main course for them is simply starters for their women.

Breaking it down for these men is as hard as telling an artist that what he thought was a masterpiece is simply crap. A large number of sistas find that it's easier making sounds like 'Ooh! Aah! Oooooh! Aah!' and 'Yes! Yes!! Yes!!!' And the easiest lie to tell, (at speed) is 'I'm coming! I'm coming! I'm coming!' No wonder selfish men are lulled into a false sense of security, thinking they are constantly holding their positions in the 'Demon Lovers' League.'

Marcia had always maintained that women had left it too late to tell their men that their tongues are one of the most sort-after parts of their anatomy. And some men who know spend too much time contemplating the consequences: 'What if she told someone I did that shit?' 'What if she felt she had something over me?' 'What if I got black grass stuck in my teeth from all that grazing?' Shit.

In the past, Marcia had considered giving the book 'How To Give Your Woman An Orgasm' as birthday presents to her men, but decided against it. Men's prides are like eggshells. Be anything less than sensitive with them, and the yolks of their egos would be all over your conscience like crapulence daubed on the walls of a madhouse. For life.

So Marcia found Conteh and was pleased. The arrangement suited him fine, and after all, how could he resist. The lady was classy, rich, beautiful, raunchy and certainly knew how to make a brother want more. Besides, he knew things would be safe with this chick. She wanted no ties, no commitment and no promises. He knew where he was at with her, and vice versa. She was down with the easy ride, not looking to upset his mango cart.

On the phone, Conteh filled Marcia's ears with "The person you're trying to call is not available, please try later," and followed his elegant wife upstairs. Sexual thoughts filled his mind, as hot as the water that rained down on his wife's naked body in the shower. Macho took backstage. He weakened, for he needed to touch her, embrace, caress and lose himself in her. Whatever else was happening in his life, he didn't want to lose her. Other women could and would wait.

After catching a quick fresh after hers, he walked slowly into the bedroom that was once theirs, and gazed longingly, with wicked passion on his mind, at the red silk sheets and her naked body upon them, as she lay dozing. He was lusting wickedly for her. It felt strange. Like he was a stranger, invading her privacy.

It had been three months and three days, to be precise, since they had enjoyed each other. Conteh was experiencing withdrawal symptoms big time. No woman compared to his beautiful wife. To him, she was the best. He couldn't explain it. All he knew was that she was his soul mate, and he feared that, if she left him, he would search forever for that feeling.

In his robe pocket, Conteh felt the wedding ring that she had thrown in his face when she found out about Evadney. He figured on putting it back where he thought it belonged.

For old times sake, he took the liberty to stretch down beside her, across the bed that was once theirs. In the past when things got cold between them, they would sleep with a wide gap in the middle, with Simone repelling Conteh's every advance (his toes accidentally on purpose wondering across the hostile threshold of their king-size bed, daring to caress hers, and nonsense like that).

Simone was somewhat startled. After all, it had been over three months since he had even attempted anything like that. She had seriously thought he had accepted the situation.

She opened her eyes slowly. Looked at Conteh with a grimace. She gathered herself quickly, posed her unwrapped 36-24-36 at him questioningly, grabbed a towel to shield her body from his gaze, and said, "Conteh, why are you in here?"

"Sure you know, baby," he said in a tone that made Simone wince. That calm, coaxing, 'Barry White' tone that she had once found hard to resist. "Simone, baby. How much longer?" He gripped the wedding ring in his pocket. "Don't you think I've suffered enough? Are we gonna try to work this thing out? Christ, I said I was sorry. It'll never happen again. Believe me. Jah know, mi luv yuh bad." He sounded desperate.

His robe was open, exposing his muscular chest.

Admittedly the brotha looked good. Simone had to give him that. As much as she despised him, he was goods enough to eat.

She knew that he loved her, despite everything. Had always known, even when she was lulled into that false sense of security that the fish she had caught and fried, would stay on her plate forever. But now she couldn't help questioning the meaning of love. If he could only stop lusting after other women.

Of course, she knew nothing about the strange woman last night. Nor did she know anything about the long standing 'dick thing' with Marcia, the rich bitch in Solihull. She didn't know that he was still sleeping with at least three of his baby mothers — Joya, Carmen and Collette — and a few other unimportant bits on the side. She couldn't be sure, but she hoped that Evadney was the only one.

"It'll never happen again," he bleated sincerely with puppy dog eyes.

"For heaven's sake, Conteh," she muttered in a low growl. "I don't want to talk about it again. We've been through this before. I want nothing more to do with you. I'll leave you to the mercy of the next woman who will be stupid enough to trust you. And, by the way, I've filed for a divorce. You'll be hearing from my solicitor."

A picture of doom gathered about Conteh. His eyes widened as he said, "You what!? Simone, you can't do this to me. You know how much I love you." Desperation decorated his tone more than before.

"Yes, Conteh, I know. You loved me all the times you cheated on me. I suppose you love me and all the bitches that are willing to accommodate your hungry manhood. Just leave it, will you? A leopard never changes its spots. I knew you were no angel when we met, but I figured love could change things. I guess I figured wrong."

Simone found her robe and slipped it on. She sat in front of the mirror, her back towards him. Why was he in her space, in nothing but his robe and revealing his sexy chest, she wondered.

Now she could feel the tension and the reflection of his approaching image forced her to stiffen. Of course, she could have moved but her emotions were now fighting against each other.

"Simone, baby, don't do this to me, please."

Gentle, yet firm, he forced himself against her back, and held her with heightened desperation. She felt the firmness of his grasp around her waist.

In the eyes of some, it would be seen as rape, for his advances were certainly unwanted. Lechery overcame him, and as he recalled how long it had been since he had caressed the firm lumps of flesh that hung so gracefully from her chest. His temperature rose. Simone could now feel his hard manhood against her back and his moist tongue was now descending down her ears. She tried to push him off, but he gripped her tighter.

"You know how much I want us to have a baby, Simone," he said, nibbling her ears, her neck, her breast. "Please, babes, let's not talk divorce. You know I couldn't live without you."

The more she struggled to push him away, the more he tried to weaken her.

"Get your hands off me!" she lashed out.

"Simone, I can't, baby. I love you. Need you. Want you." Conteh's voice was now a whisper, yet his grip was hostile. Strong.

Simone looked into his eyes. It would help if she well and truly hated him, but somehow he still had a hold on her.

"Fuck you, Conteh!" she hissed. "Fuck you," she repeated, but now in a muffled sound, as they devoured each other's mouths, wildly.

The red silk sheets now received their bodies. Simone's defences were well and truly down as the memory of how good it really was came rushing back. The warmth of his tongue against her black nipples were fully welcomed and sent ecstatic sensations through her body. The sheer heaviness beckoned tears from her ebony eyes. Now there was no turning back. She had succumbed once again to his touch. Like a boomerang, she bounced back across that thin line between love and hate.

As he kissed and caressed every inch of her body, she moaned and groaned. Simone was already in her heavens when she felt it. That moist movement against her clitoris, like a lustful snail, sweetly tingling, sweetly pulling at the inside of her lower body, the ultimate pleasure she so longed to experience again.

Conteh was on a mission and he was giving his all. He knew what his woman liked, and today there were to be no rations. *Feh real.*

Conteh was a connoisseur in the game. The under-table business that was a big taboo among his idrins (or so they claimed), was a must for him. He knew what pleasure it gave women, not just Simone, and had no hang-ups on giving pleasure where it was appreciated. According to his idrins, eating under the table was sacrilege, nasty and forbidden. It was the topic of choice at barber shops, domino parlours and pattie shops. Conteh had had countless conversations about brothas and sistas who performed such an act, and had to listen to wild and diverse opinions on the subject. Anyone who was in favour of it was condemned as, 'giving in too much to European ideas.' With this strong condemnation hanging over it, black men who dared to partake kept this part of their lovemaking to themselves. In any event, it was much easier for men to admit the receiving than the giving. 'I party, but I don't partake.' Men would nod their heads and echo their own statements of disapproval, and some would laugh nervously and take no part in the conversation, especially if their women happened to be present at the time.

Conteh gave generously. Simone could wait no longer. Her aching body longed wickedly for him to enter her, but as he hastened to help his eager, throbbing manhood inside her, her head ruled her passion and she wised up to reality.

"Condom, Conteh, condom. I can't sleep with you without one."

Conteh slowed up. This was one of the moments he despised. Sex wasn't sex if he had to wrap his manhood. Skin-to-skin was the thing. AIDS was something that happened to other people. Riding bare-backed was the lick. Only last night he had had unprotected sex with someone he had known for less than two hours. The thought that he could be putting his wife at risk had eluded him.

"Christ, babes, this is such a passion killer." A muffled protestation filled Simone's ears as Conteh reluctantly released her in an attempt to search for a rubber. He wanted to say, 'If you try and eat a mango with its skin on, you never get the true flavour,' but didn't want to risk it.

Extra sensitive condoms came to the rescue. It wasn't long before he was inside her. Heaven came down and the sheer hell of the past was forgotten. Memories of his deception invaded her ecstacy, but only for a fleeting moment.

"For crissake woman, can't you see you're my world?" said Conteh when the passion had subsided.

"I'm your world, yet you crave the world of women?" she puzzled.

Simone was sexy. Other men craved her attention and Conteh knew it. She was passionate, too, and he wondered whether she had abstained from temptation in the three months since he had touched her. He knew that women who had been cheated on sometimes sleep with other men as a way of getting their own back.

Although it burned a dirty great hole in his heart, Conteh didn't feel he had the right to ask her anything along those lines. Right then, he simply felt grateful. Holding her again seemed like heaven, and from the depth of his black ass, he pledged never to lose her again. Like all the other times, he meant it. But as sure as the sun would rise in Jamaica, Conteh was doomed to fail. His sex drive was always in overdrive.

They lay in harmony, their bodies entwined. Once again, Conteh had won.

Simone questioned her self-esteem again and searched for reasons why a woman like her would stay for more. Like so many other women, she didn't know the answer — so she called it love.

Joya, Carmen, and Collette, Conteh's baby mothers, called it love too. They called *him* Mr Soon Come. Their children were spitting images of him and would be constant reminders for life.

These women had come to settle for a mere three or four hours per month each with Conteh. Time which was divided equally between (not necessarily in this order) quality time with junior, giving 'agony' and unloading his chest with revelations like "T'ings not right a yard" and "Me an' Simone are splitting up. Soon, y'know." It was puzzling why he had to tell such tall tales, since he would get his t'ings anyway. He figured that telling them that things weren't right on the home front would make it feel right. He wanted to make each woman feel like they were really the one and that it was only due to circumstances why he didn't marry them in the first place. After all, he reasoned, they were his baby mothers, and it was better for all concerned that they remained bits on the side from one year to the next, giving their all and getting a monthly thrill in return.

Joya, Carmen and Colette all knew of each other. They hated each other for sharing the same knowledge — Conteh's dick — and would cut their eyes long and hard at each other whenever they came into contact. The hate they had for Conteh they turned on each other, leaving him unscathed.

Joya reckoned she was queen since she was under the impression that she had produced his first child. She dumped him when she heard on the grapevine that Carmen was pregnant, who in turn did the same when she found out that Collette was pregnant at the same time. However, it wasn't long before Conteh succeeded in charming his way back into their beds.

The baby mothers were caught in a trap. At the best of times, it is hard to find a man who is willing to commit to a serious relationship. Moreover, finding a man who is willing to take on the responsibility of another man's child you were virtually searching for the proverbial needle in a haystack. Joya, Carmen and Collette had all tried to make it without Conteh, but realised now that their best chance of avoiding a lifetime of fruitless relationships, was to stick to the father of their children. There were no shortage of just-passing-through men, helping themselves to the eager hospitality of these women. Baby mother or no baby mother, if a woman's got a cosy pad and a table under which a man can relax his feet, men will hang their hats for a while. At least long enough for the novelty to wear off, then they would slip back to their own trail of baby mothers in the turmoil an confusion of trying to find real love.

Loneliness has a way of making women, who have come to the conclusion that there is no such thing as Mr. Right, sentimental about their baby fathers.

"Listen, Conteh," Simone looked into the eyes of the loveable bastard. "I know I've said this a million times before, but this time it's for real. I'm gonna give you one last chance. Hurt me again and I'm out of here. I wouldn't even contemplate living under the same roof as you. I swear to God. It's a promise, Conteh."

More than last time, Conteh believed her. He held her closer, squeezed her ass, kissed her face and said nothing. For now he was pleased that she would abandon the divorce proceedings. Together they sunk into a sweet after-sex sleep and it was almost as if they had never been apart.

THREE

Pam paced for at least half an hour up and down the ramp, outside the popular eats where she had planned to meet her best mate. Simone had never let her down before. She had tried calling, but her answerphone was constantly clicking in. She would wait five more minutes, she decided.

They first met last July. The stopover flight from Birmingham International had touched down on schedule in Orlando. The girls had off-loaded their passengers and had shopped till they almost dropped. It was in the hotel bar that night that they chatted non-stop, after discovering that their parents were originally from the same parish in Jamaica — St. Catherine. Well, both Simone's parents. Pam's mother was blonde and Welsh.

Pam was beautiful. The strong features of her Jamaican father dominated the delicate features of her mother. Her short-cropped hair complimented her dark velvety complexion. She had her mother's eyes — a light green, that, she often had to explain, weren't contact lenses.

A special friendship developed between the girls, and even through all the girlie bitchiness between stewards and stewardesses alike, and even through the test of standbys, repugnant customers, trolleys and duty frees, their friendship stood its ground.

Simone didn't care too much for the jet-setting lifestyle.

It cut too much into her personal life. Pam, however was the opposite. She was single and it suited her. The girl just wanted to have fun.

Now Pam saw her as she made her way through the thick Saturday crowd that ebbed and flowed up and down the ramp leading to and from the Bullring shopping centre. She wore a black crew neck jumper over a pair of Armani jeans, and a slinky gold chain that emphasised her slender neck. Her hair, freshly relaxed, laid easy on her square shoulders, through the hustle and bustle of frantic Brummie shoppers, she displayed her usual cool, calm and collected air.

"Where have you been, girl?" Pam said with relief.

"Long story," explained Simone. "Sorry. I couldn't get through to your mobile when I tried."

"Long story? Long and hard I expect. You're glowing. Has he got a brother?"

Pam's anxiety prompted Simone to say, "Just Conteh."

"You've made up then? I must meet this irresistible Conteh. He must have diamonds in his balls for you to forgive him after last time. Come on. Tell me all about it over a coffee," demanded Pam, taking her mate's hand to negotiate the thick crowd.

Seated in a cosy corner of an old-style Italian patisserie, the girls chatted non-stop. Pam was pleased to see her friend so radiant again. The difference was immense. Simone spoke of the reunion she had had with Conteh only hours before, and how she was going to stop the divorce proceedings.

"It's nice to see a real smile on your face again, girl. You deserve to be happy. I'm happy for you, but I hope that husband of yours don't mess up again this time. I'll personally rip his balls out myself." Pam was flippant, but deep down she would if she could. She had seen the effect of Simone's broken heart over the last few months.

"Pam, believe me. This is the last chance." Simone looked a serious look into her mate's eyes.

"You deserve better, Simone. Much better." Pam was firm. She may herself have been a good-time girl, but she respected Simone for being a one-man woman.

Pam changed the subject, hastening to tell Simone of her recent rendezvous with a stranger in a multi-storey car park. She had locked herself out of her car and a tall, dark, handsome stranger became her 'knight in fashionable Reebok.' After using his expertise to gain access to her car, Pam thanked the irresistible stranger in kind. Her gratitude was generous, more than a quick one, without regards for the probing security camera and the occasional passer-by.

"He was wicked," Pam added at the end of her story.

"Pam, you're crazy, girl. What about protection? You didn't know anything about this guy."

"Listen, girl, protection was the last thing on my mind. Before we knew it, we were both smothered by the heat of the moment." Pam was flippant. "I tell you, girl, I've had a few, but this one had the wickedest slam."

"Pam, darling, this is not a lecture, but it's not a joke either. You must use a condom if you must live so dangerously. I always use one with Conteh, and he's my husband. There is no guarantee that he will keep his promise of fidelity."

Pam listened to her best mate's words of righteousness and smiled. She knew she was right, but took it with a pinch of salt. She loved living dangerously and made no bones about it.

"We're all gonna die anyway," she chuckled, "Rather than die from the food we eat, the air we breathe or even in a plane crash, why not die from the pleasures of sex?"

Simone was used to her friends playful nonsense.

The mile-high club was a reality for Pam. On more than one occasion she had found herself having it off with some fresh young first-officer on a transatlantic flight in the squashed confinement of an aircraft loo. Simone would listen to her stories and feel the cold sweat, almost as if it was she. Simone remembered the sordid details of a rich Japanese passenger who took Pam to heaven and back on a flight to Paris. He was with his wife at the time, and Mrs Kazumo couldn't help noticing the sparkle in her husband's eyes every time Pam walked by their first class compartment. Less than an hour before, Mr Kazumo had performed oriental cunnilingus on the beautiful stewardess.

"Anyway," continued Pam, "if that husband of yours messes up again, I think you should seriously consider taking up Captain Ryce on his offer to wine and dine you, girl. You know how some white men are about tasting exotic fruits and all that. You know how much he adores you. Talk about handsome. I would have fucked him long time if he'd shown the slightest bit of interest. He's looking for a lady and I suppose he knows I'm not one."

"Can you imagine Conteh's reaction if I left him for a white man? You know how black men are. Love white women but hate the idea of their black women going over to white men. They would not admit it, but it's a fact. I'm yet to find out what their logic is."

"Tell me about it, girl," said Pam. "But why should you worry about Conteh's feelings? Did he ever worry about yours in the past? You're too loyal for your own good. Simone, you deserve to be treated like the lady you are and to be respected like one. Captain Ryce is for real girl. Trust me."

There was no doubt in Simone's mind that Pam felt that she ought to kick her husband to the curb. As for Captain Ryce, Simone had often said that if she was into white guys, he would be the first on her list.

But then there was Captain Hendricks. Captain Lawrence Hendricks. The Antiguan who did it all for her without knowing it. Simone was always one for looking at the menu, but made sure she always ate at home. Lawrence was relocated from Manchester airport a few months after she met Conteh. 'Perhaps one day,' she thought. Perhaps.

Conteh wasn't always wicked in bed. There was a time when he had no idea what love-making was all about. 'In-out shake it all about' and 'wham bam, thank you mam' was once his idea of satisfaction, and when this would result in him fathering several children, he figured he was 'De man.'

But he had not told Simone, or any of his other women

how it really happened — how he really became a man that is. Figured it was best left. It wasn't through reading books, or watching videos, but by real-life lessons.

He was twenty years old and still wham-bamming, when he met Maggie, a thirty-five-year-old who was experienced to the core, and open-minded with it. Maggie was a Londoner. She had served a host of rich men behind closed doors in high-class hotel rooms in London. If they had money and wanted her service, Maggie would render it.

Conteh knew nothing of Maggie's past at first, and however it happened, he found himself between the sheets with her. Red Silk sheets.

The love doctress realised that Conteh wasn't all that, and took to giving him lessons in lovemaking. She had swallowed, it seemed, a whole volume of _The Art of Karma Sutra_, and volumes of _The Art of Lovemaking_. Like it was her duty to know.

Between red silk sheets Maggie showed Conteh how, where, why and when to touch. She taught him the secrets of a woman's body. "Going straight for the kill did nothing for a woman," she had told him. "She needs to be aroused. A woman is like a rose, and should be handled like one. She must be nurtured with passion before she could be expected to bloom. She must be tended with care too. If she is not, she could turn into a prickly thorn." As she spoke, Maggie administered touches, bringing sensational awareness to parts of Conteh's body that he had not dreamt possible.

Conteh lay there speechless. No words for the ecstasy

he felt. And if there were — no space in his throat for them to escape. Choking on ecstasy.

This woman was something.

'A devil woman,' Gladys would say.

For the first time in his life, Conteh realised that his women must have been left twitching for satisfaction. Like a dying fish. Twitching, when all he did was rolled over and slept.

Conteh was a diligent scholar, and from the classroom of love, he had developed a fetish. It fastened itself to the walls of his subconscious. A fetish for Red silk sheets. But the part where a woman is like a rose seemed to have eluded him totally.

'Settling down would take a miracle,' his mother would say. So when he told her that he was getting married, she was full of joy. Gladys gloried and hallelujahed, then set to making preparations for the event she thought was never going to happen. Gladys had made it clear that she didn't approve of the giddy-headed girls Conteh was messing with before. When he lived at home, these females used to call the house all hours, disturbing her peace and breaking into her prayer sessions, and even at the end of a telephone line, she reckoned she could detect their virtue. She would say, 'I don't know why, but mi spirit cyaan tek dat one." She had always relied on her spiritual intuitions.

Simone had her fair share of dirty looks from his exes, but they were taken with a pinch of salt. She knew all about a woman's scorn and didn't let any of it worry her.

"Why do we spend our time talking about men

anyway," Simone said, as she sipped on a coffee.

"Because we can't live with the bastards and we can't live without them," Pam replied.

Nico was rendered 'lust sick' yet again. Another Jazz night at Scottie's and a choice of easy-to-get women had made it so. The charming, smartly dressed Jamaican Indian used his looks and charm to screw his way through umpteen women. Black women who even in the new millennium tripped on the philosophy that having a coolie baby is the best thing since ackee and salt fish, and white women who figured every dark dick is filled with exotic juices.

Nico had it going on in more ways than one and he knew it too well. Lately he sported a skin-fade with a ruffled top. Tony at Frizzy Lizzy's, the wickedest barber in Birmingham, had done his scissors 'n shears act and it had added something Nico's already sexy aura and he certainly wasn't complaining.

This time it was a blonde, who, had she remembered to put the rest of her clothes on, might have been fully dressed. She was sat on a high stool, legs crossed, talking to the bartender. A cigarette projected from between her long painted nails and she held her glass with confidence. The red slit of material she wore for a skirt tried desperately to cover her black knickers. Nico was pleased. Pleased he wouldn't have to work too hard. If there was anything that pissed him off seriously, it was easy lays who made laying hard, by squeezing their fannies into tight apparels, which clasped their crutches with fasteners like Fort Knox. Nico thought nothing of ripping the damned things off — when the gift of gentry was being given out, he missed out big time — but he wasn't suffering for it. He had watched enough romantic movies and could act his way into any situation, if it was so warranted. There were 'nuff out there falling for his corny performance, he figured he shouldn't have to sweat for it. 'Nuff women coming back for more.

Tonight, however, it was certain that he'd be getting his inside leg in, even if he didn't get his outside leg over. He had only just traded in his old ride for a huge sports utility vehicle with darkened windows, and had not yet tried it for legroom.

"Shall we go somewhere where you could hear me think?"

He was now sat opposite the half-dressed babe at the bar, staring up her see-through knickers. There was method in her madness.

"I can hear your thoughts clearly from here, believe me." The blonde flicked her hair, pushed out her already protruding bosom, and dragged stylishly on her cigarette, sinking her thumbnail into its tip, like she was making some kind of non-verbal statement.

"What am I thinking then, Tracy?"

"Funny. My name isn't Tracy. It's Sharon."

"Close. Very close." Nico laughed again, showing perfect white teeth and dimples a woman would die for.

"Who are you with, Sharon?"

"Why? Do I look as if I need protection?"

"Not at all. It's just that ladies usually travel in pairs or a crowd." Nico took a sip of his drink, peering at the meeting of Sharon's thighs. There was only one thing on his mind. The one thing that had been a fixture ever since he could remember gaining sense.

"I'm on my own. Are you sure you haven't got a problem with that?" She dragged on her nicotine stick again.

"No, not at all," Nico hastened to assure her. "Can I get you a drink?"

"No. I'm fine." She glanced at her half-filled glass of vodka and coke.

"So what do you do when you're not hanging around in bars, Sharon?" Nico asked.

"I work as a journalist for a magazine in town. Gathering info is what I do best."

"Yeah? Wanna gather some a' dis?" Nico mumbled under his breath.

"Excuse me?"

"I said, don't you think it's hot in here, Sharon? Fancy some fresh air?" Nico was a fast mover. As fast as the testosterone rush that had him bubbling like a black woman's pot.

"I don't mind," she uncrossed her legs and sipped her drink. "What's your name anyway?"

"Nico." He stretched his right hand towards her.

"I hope I'll be pleased to meet you, Nico," she said, taking his warm palm inside hers.

The near-naked leggy blonde followed the hot-blooded hunk outside.

"Have you got a fella, Sharon?" Nico asked, still smirkin as they reached outside.

"A few." She flicked her hair again and inhaled more nicotine.

"Bit of a fun girl are we?" Nico was now walking casually towards his SUV.

"Why not. Why should men have all the fun? I haven't met a man yet who knew the meaning of being faithful. My heart has been broken so many times, I figured if a girl can't beat 'em, then why not join 'em. My boss is a tough black woman. I have to work hard, so at weekends I play hard."

Nico dropped back slightly, just enough to catch a better glimpse of Sharon's rear end. Her long bronze legs made him hotter. She could have done with a bit more ass, he thought, but everything else made up for it.

Sharon continued. "The last serious relationship I had was with a Jamaican guy. Well Jam-English I should say. He was born here, but his parents are Jamaicans. He would always insist he was a Jam-English, as opposed to being British. Before that it was a Barbadian and before that it was a guy from St. Kitts. They all promised me the earth. Not that I expected it."

"What happened? Didn't they deliver the goods?" Nico got a word in.

"I caught one in bed with another fella I thought was my close friend. One of them was married to three other women. Another one ripped me off and disappeared, and I discovered that one of them had twenty-four children by twenty--three different women. The sad thing about it is, I was really in love with this one. I was gutted. I knew there was something funny, but not to that extreme. When I confronted him, he simply kissed his teeth (you know how black guys do), and drove off. I never saw him again. I remember thinking if I had the chance to fuck him up I would. Now? I trust no one. All I want from a man now is an orgasm."

Nico was blown by this woman's honesty. Her openness was 'dark, man', he was thinking. He couldn't help remembering Conteh's Marcia — Just a dick thing.

"Bajan, Kitician and Jamaican, eh?" The question on his mind was, which one of them was caught in bed with another fella? "Like a bit a black then, Sharon?"

"Yes. I can't say no to that. But it's nothing to do with all that myth about what black men have in their pants, how good they are in bed or anything like that. I suppose I started dating black men because I knew it would piss my parents off. When I was young, my parents always used to warn me about going out with black men. I was only sixteen when I lost my virginity to a guy called Errol. I must admit, forbidden fruits are sweeter, but that's not every white woman's reason. We seem to have gained a reputation for craving black men for the reputed size of their sexual organs. Let's face it, I've seen a few oversized dicks that could make a horse jealous, but, at the same time, I've seen shameful ones. Just like I've met men with small organs who are wicked in bed, and some with large ones who are shamefully crap." Sharon took the last drag of her cigarette, threw it on the ground and squashed it with her right foot. "It's not what you've got, it's how you use it. Right?" She looked directly at Nico.

Nico laughed. It felt like he'd known her a lifetime

instead of minutes. He liked her style. Of course, she wasn't the type of woman he'd take home to his mother, but she was the type who would fit nicely into his current lifestyle.

"Ever had a Jamaican Indian before, Sharon?" Nico asked, with a glint in his eye. They were leaning up against his SUV on the side street. He flicked the central locking off.

"No, but there's always a first time. As long as you've got stamina, you can press my button any time, Nico." She flicked her hair and licked her thin pink lips, freaking Nico out even more when she pressed her groin up against his manhood, pulled his head towards her and damned near lost her tongue down his throat. Nico returned the gesture, and squeezed her ass approvingly, almost choking on the fragrance she must have showered in.

His manhood was now throbbing so hard, it was beginning to become unbearable against his already tight trousers. Urge overcame him and with admired authority, he lifted her off her feet, threw her onto the back seat of the SUV and climbed in after her. The smell of new car leather mixing with her perfume, created an irresistible urge inside him With his right hand he released his zipper and let his dog out. The beast was hungry. 'Hawoooah!!' was his thought.

He entered her immediately, it was easy, she was practically wearing nothing. No messing around with foreplay. She felt the sturdy force of his manhood ascending sweetly inside her. Still she devoured his mouth and gyrated her hips as if they were in competition with his thrusts.

They had been going for a while when she emitted loud ecstatic moans.

After the copulating pair had detached themselves from each other, Nico fumbled for his keys.

"Sharon, you are really something," he said, admiringly.

"You're not so bad yourself, Nico. We should do this again sometime. Besides, if you're partial to a bit more than two-in-a-bed, I can arrange something. I've got a friend who's game.

Nico was freaked even more. This woman had no inhibitions! All his christmases were coming together all at once.

"Call me," she said, slipping a card in Nico's hand and pulled on the door handle.

"Woah! Not so fast." Nico pulled firmly on Sharon's wrist. You can't leave me like this. I'm still hot. I'll burst my bank in a minute. I need me a reservoir." It was as if the thought of an orgy gave him wings. Sharon pressed her hands against Nico's un-eroding rock as if to assure herself. It was as hard as it was when she first felt it inside her.

"Sizzling or what!" she said, kissing him passionately, undoing the buttons of his shirt at the same time. Nico lowered the seats in anticipation. As the palm of her left hand handled his manhood with expertise, Sharon licked his hairy chest all over. Sliding her tongue slowly down past his navel, she tenderly kissed his sensitive bellybutton, stirring butterflies in his lower body. He was filled with wanting, and hoped she would do the ultimate deed.

His wish was granted. He was nearly driven out of his mind when he felt her warm moist mouth firmly wrapping the head of his manhood. As she licked with ravenous hunger, her moans echoing her excitement, Nico shook with pleasure. Now, moving her hands firmly up and down his sturdy shaft, she teased his head with her tongue, quickly licking, and then pulling away in spasms. She teased wickedly, and when he was almost out of his mind, she took the whole length of his now throbbing manhood into her mouth and moved her head up and down with unbelievable speed. Sharon was undoubtedly an expert, and pulled her head away just before the falls of Niagara.

Sure he had had heads before, but this was the business. 'This woman has re-invented oral sex, for sure,' he thought. He had to see this chick again, sooner rather than later, and preferably with that friend of hers.

He was still floating when he dialled Conteh's number, to run the idea of a foursome by him. Nico was Conteh's sidekick, best buddy and deep-rooted idrin. At the age of thirty-five, he was a confirmed bachelor, but most certainly not an eligible one. Had he been a woman, his reputation would have been atrocious. It was rumoured that once, whilst he was under the influence of drink, marijuana and sexual needs, he found himself between the sheets with someone he thought was a sexy blonde, until a stiff lump of flesh throbbed against the opening of his ass.

Simone had always blamed Nico for being a bad

influence on Conteh, but if the truth be known, both men were two peas in the same pod.

Conteh claimed he was different because he didn't have as many illegitimate children as Nico. His seven — well the seven he owned and claimed to know about, were nowhere near as many as Nico's tribe.

His past women were piqued at his decision to marry, and wondered what Simone had that they didn't.

"So wha'? Yuh get anyt'ing las' night?" Conteh asked casually as he lifted weights.

"Twice, star. One gyal in de cyar an' another one back at her place." Nico panted as the jogger came to a slow halt. "You remember dat chick from Smethwick? Joyce. The one who was always playing hard-to-get?" He sucked his teeth long and hard. "Full up ar' head wid one bag a con'. Yuh shoulda 'ear de gyal bawl to raas."

"Wha? A yuh dat bredrin? Bumboclaat," sang Conteh mischievously.

"So wha' 'bout you?" asked Nico.

"Yeah, man. Mitsi."

"Redskin Mitsi?" Nico sounded surprised. Only because he wanted to comb that ass himself. "Yuh lie!"

"Yeah, man, redskin, batty-barely-cover Mitsi. Sweet nuh raas," Conteh assured him. The men laughed and so did half the gym. It was an all-male section. Someone pumped up the volume on a ghetto blaster they had come equipped with, and Conteh and Nico joined in with the airwaves to sing:

Big t'ings a gwaan, yuh no see-ee-ee
Yuh no see wi 'ave de gyal dem we-ee-ak

Sexy Mitsi an' de one name Joyce
Seh dem love how wi dweet
Yuh no see a pure niceness a' dweet
Woman a get mad an' all a tear up sheet
Woman want de lovin' seven days a de week
Chew wi a good fuck, an' man wi know how fi turn on de heat
No gyal outta road cyaan seh wi luv sleep
An' nobody cyaan seh dem eva ketch wi a' creep
Gyal luv wi style chew wi always neat
Dem waan drive up inna de Lexus Jeep, (Sing Along)..

Nico caught sight of a large woman walking past the door of the gym. "Bredrin, check out dat big t'ing deh. Bwoy, dat would bruk yuh back t'rahtid."

"Feh real. Mouse on a one-dollar bread to raas."

Conteh encouraged him. They both laughed and an eavesdropper sang:

"I'm t'inking, 'bout linking, de big t'ing."

If you eva pass mi room an' hear
When mi a tu'n on de heat an' a fine extra gear
Woman waan pop out every straan' a mi hair
A' rail an' a kick-up an a gwaan like a mare
When mi put in mi descent cassette
Yuh know mi nah eject till ambition select
Dis yah gear, some bwoy a' go fret
Cause if dem gyal pass de border dem aggo get ketch
Big t'ings a gwaan.

Women would have sung a different song, so to speak. Pretty it up. Made it look good. Hoping on dreams. Wishing on stars. Seeing it as a love thing.

But men are heartless. Conteh and Nico were

downright nasty. Nico however, had the decency, if you could call it that, not to take anyone down the aisle in holy matrimony. He was not obligated to anyone until he had been down the aisle. .

"Bwoy, yuh cyaan seh there's any shortage of fresh pussy around. How many men did statistics say there were to one woman? Nuff man. Whole heap. If we didn't share it around, there would be lots of frustrated women around. Weh yuh seh, star?" Nico added.

"Feh real." Conteh stepped onto the jogger, picked up speed.

It was 3:15pm. He remembered that he had to pass by his mum's for dinner, and to see his Aunt Gertie who had just arrived from Jamaica. He had to drop by Joya. Junior wanted the money for those Nike trainers he had been promised, and he would only get what he called 'nagging' in his neck if he didn't show today.

"Gimme de gyal dem wid de wickedest slam, an' if yuh waan feh get de medal, yuh haffi get a slam from a real ghetto gyal…" Cruising along in his Beema, he sang along to the rude lyric that boomed out of his stereo.

FOUR

Business wasn't booming today. Apart from a few browsers and time wasters, who were simply seeking shelter from the cold more than anything else, no serious shoppers visited The Golden Touch.

All That Glitters the jewellers opposite seemed to have been pulling in more shoppers lately, and Conteh found himself having to give jewellery parties to help his weekly sales target. He figured if he couldn't bring the people to his jewellery, he would bring his jewellery to people.

It was just past seven when he made his exit from the small confines of The Golden Touch. As he pulled the metal shutters down on the front of his shop, Conteh diverted his mind to his wife. In half an hour, she would be landing at Birmingham International Airport. Her car was in for service and he promised to pick her up.

"Who was your Captain?"

The question wasn't innocent. Conteh often asked it ever since he caught hold of the fact that some high-flying blue-eyed Captain had his eyes on his gorgeous wife.

Simone scolded him with her eyes and evaded his question.

"Just wake me when we get home will you?" She reclined her seat and relaxed.

Conteh smiled, kissed her lips and put his right foot

down.

Ten minutes later, his mobile rang. It was Marcia. She was back from a fortnight in Paris and was obviously ready for her 'dick thing.'

"Whaap'n?" Conteh disguised his tone, like he was talking to an idren.

"The wife's around, eh?" Marcia caught on quickly.

"Yeah, yeah," Conteh replied.

"Am I seeing you tonight?" Marcia wanted to know.

"Doubt it. Tricky, man. Tricky."

"Tomorrow?" asked Marcia.

"Yeah, man. I'll call you."

"I'll get a bottle of bubbly and some Chinese in. Ciao." Marcia clicked off.

"A'right, Nico. Catch yuh later." Conteh spoke in the phone to the dial tone.

An idea came to him. He wondered why he hadn't thought of it before.

"What do you say to inviting all your friends to a jewellery party at the house, babes?"

She was beginning, however slight, to trust him again.

Making love in the shower was always their speciality, but today it was even more special as she told him of her thoughts on trying for a baby — that love child he had always wanted. He was pleased and showed her how much.

"But first... you've got to take an AIDS test," she said.

The taxman was after Conteh's blood and he was already

drained of every drop. His accountant had not handled his affairs right, and now Mr. Inland Revenue wanted five grand. Period. Of course he didn't have that ready cash and certainly did not want to grovel. He knew exactly where he could get five grand or more — fast.

"How you doing, babes? How was Paris?" Conteh embraced Marcia as he walked through the door of her luxury apartment. It was her second visit to Paris in the last six months. She loved the romantic city, but she loved her t'ings too, and now she was 'gagging for it' as Conteh would say.

"Tell you later," said Marcia, jumping on him and groping his balls.

He could have done with taking a breath, necking a Heineken and pulling a spliff. Chilling. Still, he knew what he was there for and didn't complain. He rose to the occasion.

Within seconds, Marcia's leather settee supported their naked bodies. They clawed wildly at each other as if they were both sex-starved. As far as Marcia was concerned, foreplay could come later. She was ravenous.

Marcia was loud when aroused and, as always, the whole neighbourhood knew that she was having an orgasm. Her moans seemed somewhat extra.

"God, I missed you," she panted now she could get a word out.

"So I noticed," Conteh reached for the after-sex spliff she had built for him, and lit up.

"C'mon, let's go into the bedroom." Marcia stood up

and tugged on his arm. She was ready for orgasm number two.

"Easy, babes. What's the hurry? Just chill, nuh man."

"Chill? What the hell's got into you Conteh? You're not trying to hold out on me or anything like that are you?"

"Easy, nuh! Cha! I'm a man, babes, not a sex machine. Gotta protect my structure."

Marcia's face was a question mark. "You've never complained before. Did something happen while I was away?" She folded her arms — with attitude.

"Not really, no," he said smugly.

"Well, something has changed," Marcia assured him. "You've never accused me of using you as a sex machine before."

"C'mon Marcia. We both agreed on this relationship being purely sexual, so it's not as if we don't know where it's at. Look…" He was going for the kill. "…It's just that lately I've been thinking about this arrangement…" He pulled in a mouth-full of ital. "…I realise that I can't keep doing this to my wife. I'm thinking of knocking this thing on the head."

"You what!" Marcia glared angrily at him.

Conteh's little mind game was working and he smirked on one side of his face. The no ties, no commitment, rich bitch was tripping on his notion of bringing her little dick thing to an end. Just the reaction he wanted. The chicken was in his yard and he would pluck its feathers. Bare.

He ducked as she swung her fist at his face. Fuming, she stormed towards the bedroom. He followed her with a cunning trick and a burning spliff.

Marcia burst into tears. He'd never seen her cry before. This was the woman who portrayed such hard disposition. The woman who made-believe that all her emotions resided only in her sex organs.

His voice was calm but stern. "Marcia. What's this? What's with the tears Babes? No ties, no commitment. Remember? I thought I could walk when I wanted to and visa-versa?"

"Then walk you bastard! Walk. I'm not stopping you."

"I can't understand it," Conteh sat on the edge of the bed. "The way you're acting, it looks like you want more than orgasms from this relationship." He was heartless. "Don't tell me you've fallen in love."

He was licking his own ass.

Conteh ducked again as an unexpected missile swirled past his head.

"I love you, you bastard! And I hate myself for letting it fucking happen. I swore I would never go there again and now look..." Each word was accompanied by a thump, a scratch, a kick.

Conteh tried hard to restrain her. "That wasn't in the deal, babes," he said. "You can't fall in love with me. You didn't want that. Just a dick thing, remember?"

Conteh knew he had won with Marcia. Game, set and match. It's true what they say — love changes everything. Now he had the handle. The lady was holding on to a sharp blade. He wanted five grand and would push for ten if possible. She wanted his love and wouldn't say no. He secretly thanked Maggie, the 'Devil woman' that took him to school. Between red silk sheets. Now the harvest had come.

"While I was in Paris I found myself thinking about you on another level. I realised I wanted more than just sex. I'm seriously in love with you. I didn't ever want to hear myself say that again."

"But you can have any man you want, you're not strapped for cash, you drive a wicked sports car, you've got beauty, sex appeal and everything. Why get hung-up on me?" He was stretching the test to the limit. Pretending it was news to him. He had surmised that she was falling for him long before she went to Paris.

"You don't understand, do you Conteh?" Marcia looked into his eyes.

He understood all right. To the max. The only thing he had to be careful about was that he didn't have a fatal attraction scenario on his hands. Her recent performance worried him slightly. He knew there was nothing so dangerous as a lovesick woman.

"Listen, Marcia. It's not just this guilt trip shit. I've got something else on my mind that I need to sort out before I can relax. I need time to cool out to sort it out. I suppose that's why I'm in a funny mood."

"And you don't want to talk about it?" She looked into his eyes again.

"Not really." He hoped she would ask him to.

"You mean you don't want to talk about it with me, right?"

"Yeah. And for sound reasons too. I've got pride. Borrowing money from a woman just isn't my style."

"Look Conteh, if you've got a cash flow problem I will

help. You know money is no problem. Just say how much you want."

"Thanks anyway, but no thanks. I've got my pride" He lied beautifully again. He hoped she wouldn't call his bluff.

"Conteh. How much? What's pride got to do with anything?"

"I'd need to borrow ten grand."

"I'll write you a cheque for twenty. And who said anything about borrowing?"

Conteh dragged on the spliff some more, a glint in his eyes as a heavy weight lifted from his shoulders.

Conteh could hardly contain himself as he watched her write out the cheque. After sorting out the taxman, he would treat Simone to a special meal and that dress she wanted, he decided, and he would treat himself to a brand new set of wheels. Have a good time. Marcia had her second and third orgasms that night and she was happy.

Gyal she a call me Missa Odini

Seh she aggo buy me a Lamborghini.

They slapped each other's palms, laughed Eddie Murphy laughs, and when Nico encouraged:

Man, gyal a run yuh dong

Ah nuh feh yuh fault

Tek ar' tek ar', ah nuh feh yuh fault!

Conteh laughed so much, he nearly wrapped his car around a man and his dog.

FIVE

The lounge hadn't been so overflowing with bodies since the day Conteh and Simone got married. Conteh was pleased. This jewellery party should prove fruitful.

Nico was pleased too. He was like a child with new toys. He feasted his eyes on the girls in an attempt to decide which one he should home in on.

Simone hosted her guests with pleasure, filling their glasses and feeding them with the usual nibbles. A blonde was giving Nico the eye and he felt sure he was well in. She was the one who pulled up in the Jaguar XRS. She was dressed in a skimpy white summer dress, which showed up her sexy figure and her bronzed skin a treat. Her Ray Bans were still a fixture above her forehead, and everything about her said money. She pinched his ass and winked seductively at him when he squeezed past her to pour himself a drink. 'I'll give you one, no problem, darling,' he was thinking. If she wanted it, she would get it. Husband most probably paying more attention to Boeing jets than rowing her boat.

The doorbell rang. Simone went to answer it.

"How you doing, darling..."

The voice sounded vaguely familiar. Conteh looked up. Shock grabbed him by the balls and was squeezing. Hard. He caught his breath as the panic attack gripped.

"Easy, star, I saw her first." Nico grinned. He had

mistaken his idrin's wide eyes and dropped jaws for a heavy dose of lust. He was far off.

Pam was the last blast from Conteh's past that he expected to see walking through his front door. She was the woman he had screwed senseless in the multi-storey car park.

"Fuck!" he said in a low, desperate tone. "What the hell am I gonna do? Jeeezas C'ris'. How fucking small can the world get? Simone's fucking girlfriend to rahtid!" He raced upstairs and out of sight to gather himself.

"Conteh? Darling?" Simone's voice made him panic more. "Come down and meet Pam," she called.

"Oh. Yeah. Right. I'll be down in a bit." Conteh tried to sound level-headed. He wiped the perspiration from his forehead, squeezed two drops of Calm on his tongue and braved it, taking long deep breaths along the way.

When he re-entered the lounge, Nico was already chirpsing Pam.

"Pam." Simone interrupted Nico's game and gently pulled her friend aside. "Sorry, Nico. Won't be a sec. Pam, meet Conteh. Conteh, meet Pam. At last you two have finally met. Get acquainted will yah, I'll just see what Carol wants."

Simone left her husband and her friend and hurried over to a brunette who was beckoning her.

If anyone were looking, they would have noticed that the handshake between Pam and Conteh stretched for a noticeable length. A long, questioning handshake. As it was, no one was. They were all busy spending their husband's money, adding to their already healthy jewellery collection.

"I can't believe It," said Pam still gripping Conteh's fingers. 'The man I told my best mate I had the wickedest slam with!' So you are the notorious, Conteh, eh? Now I understand why she annulled the divorce. Funny, we didn't exchange names when we fucked, did we? We had better things to do." She spoke with gripped teeth, and the mischief in her eyes made her more beautiful.

Simone filled Conteh's mind. He looked her way and was pleased she was otherwise engaged. He was pleased too for the music in the background that consumed Pam's words.

"This is a nightmare," said Conteh.

"No it's not." Pam was assertive. Abrupt. "Figment of your imagination. It never happened. We've just met, right? Tonight. From what I heard, you're a damn good actor. Simone is a great friend. I'll be damned if I'll let a dick come between us. It was good, but not that good."

Conteh smiled a nervous, smile as he watched Pam disappear into the conservatory. "Nice meeting you anyway," he said loud enough for everyone to hear.

He recalled just how nice it was. That first time. The memory awakened a host of movements. Down below.

"Well? Did you two get acquainted?" his wife asked. Simone and Conteh were now standing in the kitchen. Conteh had gone there to get another bottle of wine and to regain a cool composure.

"Nico and Pam are getting on like a house on fire…"

As if Conteh didn't already know.

"Yeah. Very assertive isn't she?" he said, gritting his

teeth.

She was a wicked lay too, but this was neither the time nor the place.

Nico had well and truly pulled, Conteh knew, because his spar was acting cool all evening, like the cat who nicked the cream. Conteh could do nothing but watch as his mate left with that 'wicked lay', looking as pleased as punch.

Nico had kindly offered to give her a lift home. She had taken a cab there in anticipation of a tipple or two. He had earlier slipped the Jaguar queen's mobile number into his wallet. He wasn't planning on missing out.

"You boned her last night?" Conteh was standing in Nico's bachelor pad pouring out a glass of homemade Irish Moss. The potent drink had become his daily medicine from way back when. Figured it helped his virility.

Conteh had stopped by to pick up a battery charger for his mobile and, inevitably, to receive the sordid details of Nico's latest conquest. Nico had answered the doorbell with a heavy head and wished his idrin had turned up much later. It was a heavy night and it wasn't that long since he had returned from taking Pam home.

"De gyal nearly kill me, man. She's a right sex-beast. Know her stuff nuh raas." Nico laughed out loud, holding his crotch. He was still hurting from where her teeth slipped and sunk into the head of his manhood. It was burning like hell.

"Tell me about it," Conteh added casually. "And don't I know it."

"What do you mean 'Tell me about it?' And don't you know what? 'Yuh soun' as if you've been there a'ready, man," Nico joked, not knowing that it wasn't a joke.

"Yeah, man. Hate to tell you, but the first cut was the deepest. The girl in the car park? It was her."

The men had made a pact never to bone the same woman (as they had put it). Not knowingly anyway, which is quite surprising for dogs.

"You're kidding me." Nico sat down as if he was pushed. "But she's Simone's best friend, star."

"Only found out last night though. Still, what made you think that would stop me?"

Conteh picked up his phone charger. Still laughing, he told Nico he'd link him later.

Nico needed another few hours sleep and as luck would have it, it was his day off. As he lounged on his couch slowly sinking into a slumber, he could hear his answering machine filling up. He wondered if the ladies in his life had got out of their beds with the sole intention to call him. For sure, he would be no good to any of them — at least not until the gash on his dick had healed.

"Where have you been hiding, beautiful?" Captain Hendricks had just picked up his funds for his landing fees and turned to see Simone behind him. She herself was waiting to cash in her commission card and pick up her float for the flight.

"Lawrence. Hi." She could hardly look him straight in the eyes. Are you the Captain on my flight? I though it was Captain Ryce." She peered at the flight programme she held in her hand.

"Sorry to disappoint you. Yes. I am your Captain. Captain Ryce called in sick."

"Of course you haven't disappointed me. I haven't seen you in ages. Last I heard, you were topping up your tan on the Antigua run." Simone tried to hide the sparkle in her eyes.

"Yeah." He smiled widely and his perfect white teeth looked even whiter against his jet-black skin. "So," he added, "am I gonna have my coffee milked and sugared by my favourite number one lady today?"

She proceeded to imagine herself between the sheets with him. 'No,' she thought. 'I love Conteh'.

There was trouble down at gate number 10. A drunk passenger didn't take too kindly to Simone telling him that he couldn't board the flight, since he would be a danger to himself and all on board. He had hurled his fair share of verbal abuse at her, gestured a host of non-verbal ones too, and was now coming towards her with a body riddled with pints of lager and anger.

By the time the airport police arrived, Simone had already done their job for them. Single-handedly, she restrained the drunken antagonist, and showed him what a black bimbo (his words) could do. Her self-defence classes had paid off today.

"God, you're some woman," Lawrence had caught the tail end of it all and showed his admiration. "Physically and emotionally, eh?"

"What d'you mean by that Lawrence?" Simone kept her

eyes on the drunken passenger, now sandwiched between the two boys in blue. Lawrence was implying something.

"I meant just what I said. Well, you are strong emotionally aren't you?" He seemed a bit forward today. Too forward.

"Do I take that as a question or statement, Captain?" She lifted a brow expectantly at him, then turned and went to attend her passengers. She hoped they were all much calmer than the one she had just had to deal with.

The regular Friday night at The Scratchers Yard was kicking. Through a mist of smoke from ital weeds, the usual crowd could be seen moving to the crucial sounds of Vibes Injection yet again. Father Jarvis, the King of revives was in the house. Country Boy and Stevie B were doing their things, and Teddy G, all the way from yard was putting in a special appearance. Celebrities in their own rights, the brothers had come to nice-up the dance, chat two lyrics, and make the people feel the session was worth the twenty pounds on the door.

Conteh had just returned from another crucial visit to Jamaica, with a wicked selection of bashment and revives and the sound crew were trying them out on the Birmingham followers before the sound clash spectacular in Manchester in a few weeks time.

The building vibrated from the heavy beat. Locks were flashing, baldheads were shining, funky dreds stood firm.

"Country Bwoy! Sevie B! Teddy G! Man call Faada Jarvis and de man call Conteh — Betta known as Egyptian! Nuff respec'. Me want unnuh feh big up unnuh self."

Senseh Fowl a mike MC held the mike triumphantly, and made the happy-go-lucky crowd move again.

"What's your name then?" Conteh's mouth was as close to the young girl's ears as his dick was to her groin. They had been locked tight like super glue for the past half hour.

He was Mr Vibes Injection — Egyptian — 'King Inna De Ring,' and she knew it. He had watched her refuse the advances of three separate gold-teethed ruffneck boys. He waited his turn patiently. Confidence was his middle name.

"Cerise." The young girl's voice quivered, almost as if God had asked the question. She had already climaxed all over her panties, as she fantasised about doing the real deal there and then. That would have been nothing new for Conteh. He could tell a tale or two about dancehall sex.

"Where's yuh man tonight then, Cerise?"

"Haven't got one," she squeaked like a trapped mouse.

"Wha'? A nice baby like yuh?" Conteh pulled back, leaned his head to one side and looked into the face of the pretty, young thing.

Conteh had pledged never to touch another young girl again. (a) He had young daughters of his own, and (b), the results in the past had proven tragic. It seemed a taste of his dick would send the young gals senseless. Then drastic measures had to be taken to prize them off his back.

Still, this busty juvenile was bursting with juice. She was in the harvest of her life and he was about to squeeze her — hard.

"There isn't any good men around, is there?" She chewed as if chewing gums were going out of fashion.

"I don't know. I haven't been looking," Conteh bantered.

"You are Conteh Egyptian, aren't you?"

He glanced down at her protruding bosom, took in the curves of her body. She was over seventeen, at least.

"Who tell you dat I'm Conteh Egyptian?"

"I heard a lot about you."

"Feh real? Like wha'?"

"Just lots."

"How about if we go somewhere later and you can tell Egyptian all you 'ear 'bout 'im?" He didn't believe in wasting time. It was he who once told Nico that wasting time and good lyrics on naive chicks, who were already hot for it anyway, was like getting out your best china for peasants.

It was just past midnight. The session was in full swing when Conteh informed the sound crew he would "soon come." The Vibes Injection crew were used to his antics, and would work the show without him. Cerise exchanged a few words with her giggling posse, covered her grin with her hand, then trailed behind him like a nervous kitten. She felt special. She was stepping out with Conteh Egyptian wasn't she?

He led her to the comforts of his Beema.

Cerise was young and had little to say. Just a few words were exchanged before he was rubbing his hand over her soft tender thighs. Fumbling his way towards her young privates, he felt the dampness of her underwear. Now she could feel his eager fingers manipulating her soft moist flesh. She moaned, like a baby being hushed to sleep.

Pulling gently on her bra-like top, he now had full access to her firm breasts. Like a hungry baby, he engulfed her nipples. Totally under his spell, she was driven out of her young mind and now the gentle movement of his warm tongue against her virgin clitoris took her to unbelievable limits.

And then she felt it — his manhood — parting the moist lips of her innocence. As he delved deeper into her, her cries could be heard a good way off, only no one was listening.

"Jus' cool," he mumbled, as he moved, now in slow motion.

Now he breathed like a tired panther at the end of its chase, his thoughts — 'Another one bites the dust'.

When Cerise had re-wrapped herself in the flimsy strip of material she wore for a skirt, Conteh gazed at her face through the small ray of light that struggled to make its way through the darkness, and through the limb of the protective tree under which he had settled his Beema. He had long since adjusted himself, and now he was thinking again of his own young daughters. The daughters he had fathered in his teens. The thought of them making out in the back of some car with an older man wiped him out for a few seconds. It had never bothered him to this degree before. Conscience was creeping in and he figured it was well and truly time he stopped it.

"How old are you, Cerise?" However late the question, he felt he needed to know.

"Old enough," she replied, still chewing gum.

However slack he was, of late he had found himself

battling with his conscience after doing the nasty with young girls. "Don't be stupid, man," Nico would say, "not'n nuh wrong wid giving a gal weh she want."

Conteh drove Cerise all the way to her parents' house in silence. He watched her as she fumbled for the keys to her house and finally turned them in the lock. When she had closed the door behind her, he sat for a while staring at the house. A strange feeling came over him about this girl, but not one that he could put into words.

'You're living dangerously!' Barrington Levy spoke to him at the right time.

He meditated on the words.

Conteh returned to the Scratchers Yard to find Nico attentively building a huge spliff. It seemed as if he could do with a bit more room, but the half-dressed babe that clung so eagerly to his side was hell-bent on not letting him breathe. Her face looked familiar and Conteh realized that she was a member of the posse Cerise was hanging with earlier.

Nico had been at the Scratchers Yard for the last hour and was wondering where his idrin had got to. Yaowzas were in order. On Conteh's arrival, Nico grinned and announced that a whiff of fresh pussy was in the air. He guessed what Conteh had been up to.

Cerise's friend eased up on her grip, to Nico's relief. There was going to be more than enough time to be gripping her in all the right places later.

"Where's Cerise?" the friend enquired.

"Took her home," replied Conteh.

"Hope you didn't spoil her. She was a virgin," the

friend said, giving him a questioning look.

"I didn't think there was any left," Conteh held his fist out demanding Nico's touch.

"To rahtid," said Nico touching Conteh's palm with his own.

Nico was happy. They had done this sort of thing so often in the past. This was more like the old Conteh, the Conteh he knew and loved. To him, that sort of behaviour was big, bad and manly. Unlike that other pussywhipped Conteh who couldn't check gal without something bothering him deep down.

As their bodies creased in hysteria, Conteh felt the jab of a sharp fingernail in his ribs.

"Share the joke then," a familiar voice said.

He turned and was surprised to see Beverley. He hadn't seen her since she gave up her council flat eight months ago to go to London with her wanna-be singer boyfriend. The bwoy must have been treating her real fine for she looked as fit as Chicken George's fiddle. How dare she come back to Birmingham looking so criss, when the task of fidelity was already proving so arduous.

Conteh and Beverley had had four weeks of serious passion a year ago, when Simone was on holiday in Jamaica with his sister Janet. Beverley knew he was married, but the girl just wanted to have fun, and fun was certainly what she had.

Beverley had had a crush on Conteh for a long time, and made no bones about it. She was everyone's knocking shop and Conteh figured on giving her a miss, but when she flashed her ass in front of him once too often, he thought, 'me haffi check it.'

Although Beverley was a tart, she was a wickedly sexy one who took some serious willpower to resist. Needless to say, Conteh didn't have willpower.

"Whaap'n sexy?" Conteh smiled his killer smile. Making a promise of fidelity was one thing, but keeping it was another. Of course he couldn't go up to Simone and say, 'Look, I'm a black man. It is absolutely impossible for me to give it all to you when there are so many women out there to be serviced. Understand. It's the African blood inside me. That is the one thing slavery didn't succeed in watering down — the natural desire to have more than one woman. It is our cultural surroundings that make it so unacceptable, and that is why we are made to feel like thieves when we do what we have the inborn desire to do.' How could he explain what felt so natural to him without hurting her? His sister Sandra once told him it was an illness. Something psychological that needed treating. And he had laughed and laughed, nearly laughing his head off.

"Nothing much," replied Beverley. "Still trying to find that perfect man." Beverley's white teeth sparkled.

Conteh laughed and pulled her close. "So what happen to yuh singer bwoy-fren'?" He was fishing and was sure to catch.

"Some you win, some you lose. How about you, Conteh? Still happily married to that trolley-dolly?"

"Hey! Easy, easy! I take offence to dat. She's the best."

Conteh's defensive stance gave Beverley a definite message — 'Don't fly pass yuh nest gyal.'

"Can't you take a joke?"

"I don't joke about my wife, yuh done know."

"But you're joking with your marriage."

"What's this? Becoming Miss Righteous all of a sudden, Bev?"

"Nah. I was just wondering why you are still screwing around if you love her so much. Why bother with all that 'I do' and all that 'Have and to hold' shit if you know you can't keep to it?"

"Okay, easy with the lecture, and stop pretending yuh nuh like it like dis." Conteh danced nastily, and the force and hardness of his manhood against Beverley's thigh, told her where his mind was at. "Anyway, who told you I'm still screwing around?"

"I've got eyes, Conteh. As I pulled up in my cab tonight, you were just checking out with some jailbait. Didn't look older than fourteen to me."

"Yeah. Right. I see you're still a comedian, only this joke stinks. What do you take me for… fourteen year olds." Conteh paused and reflected again over his most recent fix and was reminded of the soft succulence of the young girl's body. She was seventeen, if she was a day. Had to be. He reckoned.

"Fourteen, Conteh, or not far off anyway," Beverley insisted. "Young girls aren't like they used to be anymore. They just can't wait to be women. Still, give credit where it's due, Conteh, if she needed to learn to fuck, she couldn't have found a better teacher. You're the only man who could ever leave me feeling real satisfied."

"Less of the 'could,' I still cyan." Conteh bit gently on Beverley's earlobe and when she felt the warmth of his tongue descending inside, she squeezed his ass approvingly.

"Sure you have enough lead in yuh pencil, Mr Egyptian?" She gave his dick a friendly tug with her left hand.

"I see you waan fin' out. Dat can gwaan, yuh know, babes. Feh real." A sexy chuckle followed.

She most certainly did, on Conteh's soft leather settee that night — under the roof he shared with his lawful wedded wife. Simone was not due back until morning. Conteh would deal with the guilt later, for now lust would prevail.

He was greedy. Beverley was staying with her mother, and had made it clear that they couldn't go back there. Besides, her mother knew Conteh well. And she knew he had a wife too.

"Nice place you've got here, Conteh?" Beverley sat crossing her legs on Simone's settee. "She is beautiful too," she added. Her eyes fell on a giant-size portrait of Simone. "I could never understand men," she continued. "Have beautiful women at home, yet spend their lives chasing skirts. Always searching for something else. Why do you suppose that is, darling?"

"Don't know." Conteh handed Beverley a drink. "But I know one thing," he continued, "bitches like you don't help. Admit it. We couldn't do it without you. Take tonight for instance. You could have told me to sling my hook, but you didn't, did you? So... don't... blame... men... completely." Conteh's tone was laced with desire as he leant forward, kissing and teasing Beverley's ears. At the same time he dimmed the light by remote control and began his sordid act for the second time that night.

He wanted to impress, remind her of how lethal he could be. Especially after that 'still got lead in your pencil' comment back at the Scratcher's Yard. He hadn't forgotten how 'sucksexful' his first encounter with Beverley had been. She used his dick as a gobstopper.

"Don't your wife ever get back earlier than expected?" Beverley attempted a muffled concern.

"Don't worry. You could always sneak out the back. It'll just be a role reversal for you."

Beverley appreciated the irony. He recalled her telling him of the time her man returned earlier than expected from a weekend away. She was busy getting her welding done when she recognised the sound of his engine settling in front of the house they shared. Her lover had only enough time to leap downstairs and out the back door with his clothes and shoes under his arm, and a hard-on that would not die. She had earlier doctored his drink with a heavy dose of Spanish fly, to ensure she got what she had bargained for. Lucky for the brother, it was summer. Sub-zero temperature and the effect of Spanish fly would have surely been a recipe for rigor mortis. Beverley pretended she was fast asleep when her man walked into the bedroom. But the following morning when he found a pair of male briefs that were not his hanging out the bottom of the bed, Beverley had some serious explaining to do.

"Just a moment." Beverley pushed Conteh away gently. "Can I use your loo?"

Conteh eased up. "Top of the stairs, first door on your

left." He reached for his drink and downed it in one. The room was missing atmosphere and what with the eyes from Simone's portrait fixed firmly on him, he dimmed the light even lower than before. No sooner had he lined up a tape booming out 'Girl, I wanna sex you up,' Beverley re-entered the room wearing nothing but a pair of red thongs.

"What are we waiting for then, Egyptian? Christmas?"

Conteh rose to the occasion in more ways than one. As his wife worked her ass off in high altitude, he worked his off with a nasty attitude. He had had Beverley any which way until both their batteries ran flat and he prayed that Simone wouldn't come home in a horny mood. He had nothing left to give.

The ringing of his mobile awakened Conteh. The doze after his romp with Beverley had stretched far longer than anticipated. He opened his eyes to a shower of sunlight from the window. It was morning and he was reminded of how he came to be stretched across a nude body on the settee that his wife loved so much to relax in.

"Shit!" He jumped to his feet and shook Beverley back to consciousness. He checked his watch and found that Simone was due home in less than an hour. "Get dressed, woman!" He shouted, smacking Beverley's ass.

"Okay! Okay! Keep your dick down." Beverley stumbled to her feet and made her way upstairs to find her clothes. She felt no shame. Walking all over another woman's house in her birthday suit, as if she owned the damn place. She took her time about it, too, which made Conteh despise her.

Soon Beverley was downstairs and the little red number that looked just right in the dimness of last night, now looked rather tarty in the cold light of Saturday morning. What with the pasty look of stale foundation and lipstick that looked as if it was put on by a drunken artist, Conteh found her repulsive.

"See you later, big boy," she said as she was literally shoved out the front door. Luckily for Conteh, her taxi arrived in time. The courteous gesture of giving her a lift home was simply out of the question. He had to ensure that everything was in place before Simone's return. It wouldn't be easy. Beverley's perfume was still lingering, and the settee had acquired a new shade from her foundation.

He had to start working. Fast.

SIX

One day at a time, sweet Jesus
Tomorrow may never be mine
Help me to stay
Show me the way
One day at a time.

Gladys sang as she busied herself. Her rice and peas were teasing Conteh's nose, and when a whiff of her spicy jerk chicken wafted through to the front room, he couldn't resist getting up and sneaking a busty leg from the kitchen.

"Can't you wait," she said, catching him red-handed and giving him a playful shove.

She didn't go to church today since she had invited all the family to dinner. This was a rare occasion for Simone, since she was always so busy.

Gladys's crowded front room reminded her of her mother's, before she persuaded her to make it more modern. All it took was to get rid of some of the nostalgic cluster and to stop regarding the living room as a gallery for all the family heirlooms.

Gladys' front room was her shrine in more ways than one. To displace a single relic would be almost sacrilege. The room had seen many hours of worship and prayers and echoed with the memories of her Sonny, under the influence of firewater. There was a print of Leonardo's Last Supper. One too of the usual white Jesus. Expensive china and special glasses kept for special visitors who rarely visited. Guests like Pastor Brown and his wife, Deacon Harris, Evangelist King, Sister Ellis and the pastor's son, Vincent. Vincent more so of late, since he caught a whisper in the wind that Sandra, Conteh's younger sister, was home from university. He had had his eyes on her ever since it made sense.

Gladys thought the sun shone out of Vincent's backside and would have married them off ages ago if she had the chance. What she didn't realise, was that Sandra, living away at university, was no longer wearing a holy blinker, and seeing only church life. She had grown. She engaged in all manner of conversation. Discussed all the 'isms' 'scisms' and 'ologies' man had created. Compared evolution to the holy creation and (shock, horror) had even dabbled with atheism. She was becoming a woman of the world, who regarded Vincent as a boring old fart. "Let us pray," she would mimic him.

"Dat University has ruined you," Gladys would say. "A don't know about educating. It has brainwashed you. And look how you use to sing, an' pray an' all de members dem use to love to hear you exalt in de Lord. No wonder dem seh education is sin."

Sandra would reassure her mum that she still believed in God. And that God is everywhere. Even in universities. And that she still prayed. She would tell her that she didn't have to go to church for hours on end each Sunday to show that God was real. But it was just that Vincent needed to lighten up. Besides, she had grown out of him now. When she had her head stuck in her Bible (as she would put it), she thought he was her type, but now she realised he wasn't. Although she was yet to pinpoint her type, but it certainly wasn't Tim, the weedy little white boy who took her virginity in her digs at university. She had tried to tell Vincent straight. Several times. She couldn't bear to watch his bottom lip drop to the floor like half a pound of liver. Then he would say, "The devil is working on your mind, Sandra. Let us pray about it."

"Hi, Simone."

Sandra walked into her mum's front room and found Simone looking again at a photo of Conteh and herself and her sister Janet. Conteh was a mere six years old, Janet three and Sandra only two. This was one of the pictures Conteh often got embarrassed about, but Simone loved it to bits.

"Hi, Sandra." Simone turned towards her sister-in-law and the girls hugged.

They hadn't always clicked. She had always found Janet easier to tolerate. Before she left for university, Sandra used to make it her duty to ram the Bible down everyone's throats three times a day. Every time Conteh and Simone would turn up at the Gonzalez's house, Sandra would jump on them, Bible in hand, saying 'Shall we have a word of prayer?' Conteh would smile, hug her and say, "A'right, sis. Easy wid de lecture nuh."

Now Sandra had changed and Simone realised that they had a lot more in common than she thought.

"How's studies, girl?" Simone asked.

"Sound, man, sound." Sandra sounded more hip too. "You're looking well," she added.

"You're not looking so bad yourself, girl," Simone told her. She wouldn't tell her, though, that she wasn't keen on her freshly grown funky dreads. After all, it was her hair. Besides, Sandra would probably turn it round and start to preach to her about the downside of the chemicals black women put in their hair, and how European we have all become, and how ashamed we must be of our hair that one of our worst nightmares is our natural roots coming through. And what if they stopped manufacturing perm lotion? And did she know that it was a white man who invented perm lotion? And how in his invention, he had succeeded in convincing us that our precious Africanness needed nuff redress.

And the list would go on.

"Whaap'n, dready." Conteh walked into the room munching the last of his jerk chicken. "Yuh tu'n rasta now?"

"I see *you* haven't changed, bro'." Sandra gave her brother a hug. Taking advantage of the moment, she whispered into his ear, "Are you looking after her?"

"Yeah man. You done know." Conteh looked over at Simone and smiled.

"What have I missed?" Simone's ears pricked up.

"Talking *about* you, darling, not *to* you." He winked at her.

Simone scolded him with her eyes playfully, then picked up where she left off. She feasted her eyes again on a black and white picture of Sonny and Gladys. Gladys was slim beyond recognition. She wore a white sleeveless dress that must have been the epitome of the 50's fashion.

It nipped her waistline, emphasising a perfect figure. Her hair was rolled up in a bun and she looked like a model out of a black beauty magazine. Sonny stood by her, proud. He wore a black suit and a steady hair cut with a parting at the side. It was almost like looking at Conteh. He was dead handsome, and Simone stopped herself from resenting him again as she recalled the stories Gladys had told her about his womanising ways.

The picture told a perfect story, for it was then. Perfect. Way back when. In Jamaica. But later it had proven too extreme for words.

"How many times are you gonna look at those pictures, babes." Conteh caught the expression on Simone's face and tried to interrupt.

"I still can't get over how much like your dad you are," said Simone, now staring through the nets into the street, wishing her husband had inherited only his father's looks and not his passion for infidelity.

The doorbell rang again. Conteh went and let his sister Janet in.

"Whaap'n, sis? Mum didn't tell me you were coming. What's with the new motor? T'ings a gwaan fi yuh?" Janet wasn't fully through the door before she was bombarded with hugs and kisses from everyone.

"A'right, San'? Mmmm... don' know if I like your hair." Janet kept her eyes on her sister's funky dreads. They were always honest and open with each other.

"It's okay, darling. It's for me to like, not you," Sandra said with a wide grin.

"Serious. Serious," replied Janet. "Salaman's gran'pa

gone a' Equador, lef' 'im wife an' pickney out a door, nobody's business but 'im own." It was an old song her mother sang to them when they were much younger.

After her round of greetings, Janet found her mum in the kitchen as usual. Gladys loved cooking for her family, although she didn't do it so often of late.

"Could you pass the rice please?" Vincent gestured to Sandra as if she was a stranger. When she had greeted him earlier at the door, he damned near choke on his own breath. He hadn't realized he was staring so long and hard at her hair, until his mother nudged him discretely. And when he walked behind her to the dining room and he could see her knickers through the rips in her jeans, he wondered if she had studied so much she had flipped. Her mum had asked her to change for dinner, but Sandra simply reminded her about the 'rendering your heart and not your garment' bit in the Bible.

It would not have crossed Vincent's mind that people paid big money for jeans with holes in them. In his mind, she looked weird, wild and not all there. He would now think twice about saying, 'Let us pray,' for he thought the devil had truly won and there was no hope for Sandra now.

"It was a nice service today Sista Gonzalez. Evangelist King cyan really preach." Sister Brown tried to distract his son's attention from Sandra's hair. "De congregation really turn out today. Eh, Vincent?"

"Amen," responded Gladys, as she piled spicy chicken onto Simone's plate. Gladys doted on her daughter-in-law. Every time Simone and Conteh would show signs of breaking up, she would get down on her knees and ask the Lord to move in mysterious ways and get them back together again, and to remove Conteh's defects at the same time. And when they would make up, she would whisper to herself, 'De Lord answer prayer.'

When her dear husband, Sonny, was alive, Gladys used to tell him, 'Conteh tek after yuh. Wid yuh womanising ways.' But she hadn't ever dreamed of leaving him. Her generation was built on tolerance, or something. Something that made them forgive in abundance, and stayed together for poorer, for worst, for sickness. For till death, did her and her Sonny part.

She nursed him to the end when an unexpected stroke left him paralysed from the waist down. She would not have it any other way, for she had forgiven him for the misery he had dished her. But she did not forget that when he was young and had it in his tall dark and handsome being, he spent most of his nights with other women. She knew, for he would come home with lipstick on his collar and strands of blonde hair hanging from his head and all over his jacket. He would slur, and stagger, and kick up a fuss about the simplest thing. And when they would lie in bed at nights, when he had nothing left to give her, he would call the names of these women in his sleep and make happy, lecherous sounds. Gladys would listen and lift her eyes to the Lord and say, 'Lord, forgive him for he knows not what he does."

No, she did not forget, but she had surely forgiven, for she had seen the regret in his glazed eyeballs as she washed his helpless body, humming, 'Blessed assurance,

Jesus is mine..' She also knew that if this misfortune hadn't befallen him, and a wheel chair wasn't his only form of mobility, he would have still been staggering home drunk and smelling of strange perfume. To the end, she made him his ackee and salt fish, his yam, banana and dumplings. And his mutton soup on Saturdays wouldn't go amiss. 'Once a man twice a chile,' she would say as she rubbed La India in his hair.

And she knew what she would tell her Lord if he asked what she did with her life. Lived it on a hard-bargained promise.

Gladys always knew she would take her wedding vows to her grave. But as she poured gravy onto Simone's rice, she knew her daughter-in-law wouldn't be doing the same. And if the truth be told, as much as she loved her son, and as much as she would pray for them to stay together, she wouldn't blame Simone if she decided to leave. She knew that Simone would eventually leave him and that he would wander forever trying to find another her.

Gladys' eyes met with Conteh's across the table as he downed a glass or her delicious carrot juice. Conteh recognised the look in his mother's eyes and knew exactly what she was thinking. He looked down and she knew he understood.

There was a special bond between Conteh and his mother. They had a special mother-and-son closeness and a spiritual one too. Gladys could tell a few stories of when Conteh was a child. How he could always pick up on her emotions. He knew when she was sad even when she tried hard to hide it. There were times too, when she thought they were both telepathically in-tune. She couldn't explain it, but she knew that although she loved all her children, Conteh was extra-special to her, and was always there for her, much more than the girls.

He was there for her when a mixed race teenage boy stood on her doorstep and told her he was looking for his father. The boy was the spitting image of her Sonny, and before she could ask any questions, Gladys could feel her knees weakening and the life leaving her. When she came to, she found Conteh hovering over her, worried and fussing.

She had fainted in the face of reality.

She had always heard rumours that her husband had fathered several children by different women, but Sonny would always dismiss the stories as packs of lies. Conteh helped her through the trauma, so it puzzled her as to why he would choose to hurt Simone, after seeing the pain his own mother had gone through. She told herself that infidelity is something men just cannot help.

Gladys swore by her dreams. She was a strong believer in them, and would have meanings for the simplest ones. Called each one a vision. Whenever she would get one of her visions, and if they weren't good ones by her reckoning, she would fast and pray hard about it.

Later she would tell the family of the latest vision she had had. One she didn't like at all. She had brought the family together, with Pastor Brown, to pray — especially for Conteh.

Conteh didn't like moments like this much. He had always said his mother believed too much in dreams. He himself, (when it suited him to do so) had always put them down to 'nothing more than one's subconscious running wild as you sleep.'

They were now sitting in the crowded front room.

"I see him in a dark cave, trying hard to get out. I tried to open it but I couldn't." Gladys was looking straight at Pastor Brown, who was nodding simultaneously. "In the dream he was a bird, but his wings were clipped," she continued. "Just as I got near enough to open the cage, an invisible thing swooped down and swallow him up."

"Hallelujah!" Pastor Brown had a touch of the spirit. He didn't like the dream himself and felt it warranted prayers.

"Oh, mum. It's just a dream." Sandra dared to be herself.

"Shut up, Sandra!" Janet dug her finger into her sister's side.

Simone didn't know what to make of the whole thing, so she sat there, responding only by looking at everybody else's expression. She was covered in goosepimples, and was worried about Conteh.

Vincent held his head down and was praying. Hard.

Conteh tried to dismiss the whole thing by saying, "Mum, you worry too much." He tried too to disguise the worried look on his own face, as he remembered his own re-occurring dream, where he was always fighting with this thing that was always trying to take his life. He decided he wouldn't tell his mum. She would only worry some more. Worrying wasn't good for her, especially now she was suffering from high blood pressure. He looked at Simone and they communicated their thoughts across the room.

"Shall we pray?" requested Pastor Brown when Gladys had finished telling of her vision.

Heads were bowed, and all eyes closed, except one. One of Conteh's. It was on Simone. Figured it was okay to watch-and-pray. He did this every now and then. Stared at her as if trying to understand how it would feel if she had done to him what he was doing to her. He sometimes imagined she was. Beat her with the lashes of his own conscience. Conjure up imaginary rendezvous with Captains, First-officers and other upwardly mobile men.

Today the stare was for mixed reasons.

Conteh's mobile rang in the middle of Pastor Brown's 'In the naaaaame of Jeezus!" He rushed outside to take his call, a profane gesture they could all do without.

It was Marcia. She wondered if he could pass by later. When he told her he doubted it, she tripped. She had been tripping a lot lately and Conteh knew the ice he was treading on was wearing thinner by the day. He had had a few little funnies with her after the twenty grand donation, and he knew that there was no doubt that she was infected with a medium dose of fatal attraction, which could prove to be dangerous if he wasn't careful. Besides, he had to keep her real sweet since there were lots more where the last twenty g's came from. Not only that, she could seriously rock his marriage boat.

Although Simone hadn't the slightest idea, it was Marcia who supplied her husband with his new wardrobe filled with the latest designer gear. He didn't treat himself from the proceeds of his last sound clash spectacular like he told Simone. Marcia had done some serious shopping in Paris for her dick thing, especially when she realized that her feelings had moved to another level.

"Baby, you know it's not that easy. Especially on a Sunday night if the wife is off duty. Yes. I want you too, babes." He was experienced enough to know that words can do so much, if they were the right ones. Ones the listener wanted to hear — even if they are great big whoppers.

Conteh looked towards the sound of footsteps and saw Simone approaching. The praying session must have ended. "Later then Nico." He pretended Nico was at the end of the line. Marcia took the hint again. She was used to it, but today, she was not pleased.

"You could at least stick around to receive your prayers, Conteh. You're so rude. Why didn't you turn your mobile off?" Simone scolded.

"My prayers have been received, darling." He kissed his wife and groped her ass. "Are they finished now? You know how Pastor Brown goes on. Runs on Duracell, that man. Feh real." He would never be that flippant to his face.

"Yes, they're finished." Simone raised her brows at his blatant profanity. "But Vincent is now lecturing Sandra about her appearance," she continued. "I dare say she's giving him as good as she's getting."

Conteh laughed and they both walked back into the house. When they got there, the Browns were leaving.

"De Lord bless you, Sista G."

"Sandra, good luck in you last year at university."

"Take care, Janet."

Everyone was busy drowning themselves in formalities and etiquette.

Conteh shook Pastor Brown's hand and felt a serious surge of guilt rushed through his body. He remembered the days when he was his favourite. When he ran errands, did chores and acted as head boy, in the little Pentecostal church on the corner of Baxter Road. Now the surge of guilt was like a charge that contrasted the two men's lifestyles. He felt as if Pastor Brown could see straight through him. That he could see his sins. That he could see every one of his dirty deeds upon his face. And his mum telling him her dream didn't help much, either.

"Take care of yourself, Conteh. Don't forget to pray."

"No, Pastor, I won't."

Conteh was pleased when the pastor loosened his grip on his arm.

The whole family walked the Browns to the door and watched them climb into a gleaming Mercedes.

"Collection plate fat these days, eh mum? Billy Graham, eat your heart out, man." Conteh was full of it again now that Pastor Brown was truly gone.

"Don't be so scandalous, Conteh. What's wrong wid yuh? Yuh never tek anyt'ing serious."

Conteh loved to wind his mum up but he knew her too well not to know that today, apart from her dream, there was something else on her mind. So, when she took him aside and questioned him about his ongoing womanising, and told him she wasn't stupid and how careful he's got to be, he wasn't surprised. A church sister had caught hold of a rumour about Conteh and Marcia and brought it right home to Gladys. On top of that, her vision was worrying her beyond belief.

SEVEN

It was her ass that attracted him to her. Later he would see her face, discover her intellect and know he had found another heaven.

She had only one intention at the time — to try the diamond and sapphire ring that stood out so uniquely from the rest. She had been looking all morning without success, and now she found it under the gleaming display counter of the Golden Touch.

"Need any help?" Conteh asked anxiously.

"Yes. Can I try this ring please?"

The raunchy lady pointed to the remarkable piece of jewellery through the glass cabinet. She was assertive. She turned and caught Conteh's eyes on her backside.

"The ring is in the cabinet, not on my ass."

Conteh emitted his infamous sexy chuckle and said, "Feh real."

"I hope this is," she said.

"Come again?" Conteh was lost.

"The ring. I hope it's real."

"Oh, right. Very funny. And what comedy school have you just graduated from?" He imitated the Queen's English. He was versatile.

"Wouldn't you like to know."

The seductiveness of the lady's tone made his cock throb. He chuckled as he reached for the exquisite gem. As she examined it on her finger, he took the opportunity to examine her once more.

"It'll have to be adjusted," she said, and Conteh knew it was a sure sale. His only task now, was to try to secure a sure date with this tasty lady.

"No, problem. I like a woman who knows just what she wants."

She smiled and said, "When could I have it?"

"Anytime," he said with a glint in his eyes. "The ring I mean." He assumed he could be bright.

She glared at him half-jokingly and said, "I see you're well up on your customer service."

"Seen... You can have your ring in a week," Conteh assured her. "But I'll need a deposit." This wasn't customary, but it would ensure the lady's return.

"No problem. Here's my card. Call me when it's ready?"

"Menna Jarrett, Editor — *Black Star Magazine*." Conteh read aloud with a questioning tone, holding the business card as if it commanded nurture.

Now he wasn't so sure. Thought a lady like this would want bigger fish than him to fry. He compared her to Marcia and, although he didn't know much about her, something told him there was a clear difference on the moral front.

"Yes. Just leave a message if I'm not there," she said.

"Right," said Conteh reaching for his receipt book.

"Oh, by the way. Could I have it engraved with my initials?" she asked.

"Sure," said Conteh. Whatever you like. It's your

piece."

She smiled.

"M.J. I presume?" Conteh lifted an eyebrow.

"Yeah, that's right," Menna assured him.

Conteh handed the assertive lady the receipt for her deposit, then watched her come-to-get-me ass disappear. He needed no permission to fantasise, and did so, big time.

"Eyes off, star, she's mine."

Conteh was laying his claim. Nico had just arrived, and caught a back view of Menna departing, she climbed into a gleaming Mercedes Sports. Nico's tongue was hanging out — at both the lady and her ride.

"Remember you're supposed to be on a diet, rude bwoy. Strictly eating at home and all that, remember?" Nico reminded his mate of his promise of fidelity to Simone.

"Fuck you. She's still mine." Conteh held up Menna's business card and teased Nico.

"Okay, but if she flops you, I'm in," Nico countered.

"She'll eat you for breakfast, mate." Conteh defended his chances. "Anyway, easy with the reminder, man. I know I'm supposed to be grounded, but what's to stop me sneaking out the back door every now and then? It isn't right that God should make women so tasty, then limit us to tasting only one at a time. Nah, man, it's like looking at a plate of jerk chicken, knowing you are only allowed one tiny piece. Dat cyaan work a bloodclaat. Our African ancestors had the right idea, man. They had more than one, with no arguments. Sister-wives, man. Only wimps can be satisfied with this one woman shit."

"To raas. Wimps with limp dicks." Nico rounded off the conversation with the corny remarks then added, "Anyway, man, when are you going for that AIDS test you're due for? Remember what de wife said: No test, no love chile."

"Nico, you're one fucking reminder of doom and gloom today, man." You know, I'm not taking no raasclaat AIDS test."

"Are you off the idea of a baby with Simone then?" Nico knew how much Conteh wanted that love child. Of all the children he'd fathered, he had always said it would be the only one made from love.

"Nah, man. I don't have no AIDS. Do you see me losing weight, breaking out in spots and all that shit? I'll just tell her I've had the test and that it's negative, man. Just as long as she don't ask for written proof. You know how she stay already."

"You're on your own with dis one bredrin." Nico checked his watch indicating that he must go. "But if she find out you're lying," he continued, "I think you'll be bad flavour of the era…" He paused, glanced at his image in the security monitor, then said, "What yuh reckon' wid dis Menna, then? Think you'll fuck her?"

Nico's gold-crowned grin emphasised his barefaced rudeness.

"Is the Pope catholic? Is Kunta Kinte African?" Conteh laughed.

"Morning, young man." An old eccentric looking white woman, already dripping in gold fumbled her way into the shop. She obviously had a fetish for the precious metal, and the way she exhibited her wares around her wrinkled neck, she could not have given the slightest thought to the possibility of being mugged.

"How you doing, Mrs. Clutterbuck?" She was a regular and Conteh treated her with the respect she deserved. The respect that age and loyal custom commanded.

"Couldn't be better," she replied, her eyes wandering all over the shop.

She looked the fussy type and Nico left, giving his idrin the time he needed to deal with her.

"Later, bredrin," he said as he made his exit.

"More time, star," said Conteh, averting his attention to the old lady. But only half his attention, for just then, his mind became filled with his mother's lecture not so long ago. A surge of guilt washed over him like waves over misplaced pebbles. He knew he couldn't resist Menna. Or perhaps 'wouldn't' would be a better word.

Conteh could hardly wait a few days to call.

"Menna Jarrett." She answered on the first ring.

"Menna. Hello. It's Conteh. The Golden Touch. Your ring is ready for collection."

"Oh! Right. Thank you. I'll be down tomorrow around one. Is that okay?"

"Yes. I'll see you then."

Conteh didn't want to miss out on the opportunity. His intuition told him the wedding ring must go. He had already taken great pain in hiding it when she first visited the shop. She didn't seem the type who would go for a married man.

"Fits like a dream," Menna was pleased with her ring and as Conteh dealt with her credit card, she couldn't help noticing his band-less finger. Still, that didn't tell her much. 'It is simply a band of gold that could be removed at anytime,' she thought. Or it could mean that he was married, but not in the church sense.

She had read his mind. Figured on all his intentions. She would respond positively to his advances. After all, he was tall, dark, and handsome and upwardly mobile. He seemed like a good catch and she would certainly cast her net.

"Thanks for that, Conteh, really," Menna said through perfect white teeth.

"Like I said, it was no problem. After all, you're buying." Conteh handed Menna her receipt and credit card. "Anyway," he added, "A classy lady like you shouldn't be buying such an exquisite piece for herself. You should let the man do that.

He was fishing for clues.

"If I had one," Menna obliged. "Is that what you do for your woman? Buy her expensive exquisite pieces? Or does she just pop in and take her pick when she's ready?"

"What woman?" He looked her straight in the eyes.

"You haven't got a woman?"

"Did have. But it's all history now."

Tomorrow was another day.

"Menna. Hi. I hope you don't mind me calling."

"Conteh?"

"Yes. It is." He laughed. "How you doin'?"

"Fine. You?"

"Cool. I'm cool."

"Have I left something in your shop?" Menna asked.

"Nah, nah. Listen. I'll get straight to the point." He chuckled. "I was just wondering if you would do me the honour of letting me take you out for dinner some time?" He clenched his teeth in anticipation.

"When were you be planning on being honoured, Conteh?"

"Whenever you're free."

Conteh was casual, but really, he hoped she would choose a time when Simone was on duty.

"I'll call you."

It was her prerogative to stall.

The restaurant that Menna and Conteh sat in a week later was a dream. The Xaymaca Experience. Island paradise had come to life under one roof, in Birmingham. An amazing Muriel of Dunns River falls complimented a sugar cane scene and the image of a beach. As he gazed at Menna across the soft flame of a candle, Conteh knew that she would be more than an average fling. He already had his plate full, but the man just could not help himself. Perhaps, as his sister Sandra said, it was an illness that needed treating.

They started with the Secret Garden Combi: layer of ackee and callaloo wrapped in filo pastry case, covered with tomatoes and sweet peppers. Later, between sips of the best wine, Menna enjoyed Fish Escovitch Brean, stuffed with escallion and seasoning, while Conteh feasted on Chicken Kingston, fricassee style. There was hardly any room for dessert but they couldn't resist, so across the table, they fed each other with Banana Flambée and Crêpes Créoles.

The meal was unforgettable. Soft music and clever conversation filled the air as they got more acquainted. But that wasn't enough for Conteh. He suggested an extension to the evening. After all, right about then, his darling wife would be serving a host of hungry passengers in high altitude, and couldn't possibly know of his latest rendezvous with lust.

"Fancy a coffee to round the night off?" he asked as they pulled away from the restaurant. Menna picked up on his tactic, since there could hardly be any room left in his stomach for anything else that night.

"I don't drink coffee," she replied, smiling.

"Tea then?" joked Conteh, "Or me?"

"I'll settle for the former, thank you," agreed Menna. She would go with the flow. "As long as you realise that tea is a beverage served in a cup and not the carnal flesh served between sheets. But it'll have to be your place. Experience taught me that if a man can't take you to his place, he has something to hide. The same if he insists on giving you his mobile and not his landline telephone number. Besides, I would imagine you have the most exquisite bachelor pad in Birmingham."

Her assertive speech had Conteh stunned, and he fumbled for an answer. He had tried his best to keep off the subject of the home front back at the restaurant, but now he had come to that bridge and must cross it. He had to tread real carefully.

"Er… There's just a slight snag in that, Menna." Conteh fumbled with the buttons on his stereo and the voice of Dennis Brown intervened. Conteh knew he was making a rod for his own back, but knew he couldn't tell the truth if he wanted to get anywhere with this baby. Anywhere, meaning into her bed. "It's like this," he continued, "I live with my mother and four sisters. My mother isn't keeping good health right now. As it's late, I think it would be better if we go to your place. That is, if you don't mind."

He held his breath.

The seconds spent anticipating Menna's reaction seemed like forever. She was looking at the side of his face. He had kept it straight. Not to concentrate on the road, but to avoid eye contact.

"You live with your mother and four sisters? I just can't see it."

"Why? Should it be written in my face?"

No one had ever questioned his story before. A slight annoyance erupted in his voice. The King was sliding off his thrown. *Feh real.*

"Hey. You're not getting touchy are you?" Menna sensed his irritability and decided to go easy on him. Perhaps (she thought) his manhood was slightly dented by having to admit that he, Mr Bombastic, King-Inna-De-Ring, was still under his mother's roof, sharing a bathroom with his four sisters!

"Okay, my place," she said, giving him the benefit of the doubt. "But I hope you like herbal stuff. I never touch caffeine."

"You can de-caff me anytime, babes," Conteh was relieved and presumptuously squeezed Menna's knee. The invitation to her place seemed to have given him wings.

His Beema hugged the road and glided with a difference. Sanchez serenaded them with the sweet melody of 'I believe I can fly,' and the luxury of his prestigious ride added niceness to the journey.

Soon they were in Sutton Coldfield. The classy emanation of the lady, and the plush area reminded him of his first encounter with Marcia. The only difference was that this baby would be after more than just a dick thing. It wasn't long before they were relaxing in Menna's exquisite apartment, when earlier she had wiggled her sexy ass in front of him, his dick kicked in and pushed his brain well out of it. He was like a mouse confronted with a pile of cheese. Can't leave a morsel behind. He could murder a spliff, because it would take more than herbal tea to keep him from trying to hit that ass.

Menna stretched across her soft leather settee with her head on Conteh's lap. Gently he stroked and kissed her face. She petted his chin and penetrated his eyes and imagined what an awesome lover he would be.

"Why don't you slip into something more comfortable?" mumbled Conteh, his lips pressed against hers.

"Who said I'm not comfortable?" Menna pulled slowly away from him.

"You know what I mean," said Conteh.

"You mean, like… this?"

Conteh nearly choked on his own breath when the perfectly sculptured lady slowly peeled off the slinky little number, and had him shaking in the presence of beauty. The dim room made her look like a dream and Conteh felt lucky. It wasn't long before her Italian rug was receiving the heat of their passion.

Now Conteh figured he knew where this baby was at, and didn't waste time doing his stuff. The foreplay was sensational. Menna had climbed the wall to heaven and back, and marvelled at the man's expertise. He had touched, kissed and teased every part of her body, from her head to her toes, and now his warm tongue was manipulating her hungry woman. She ached with pleasure as he teased her, inserting his tongue with sweet force, then gently, licking, sucking and fingering her moist vagina. He was aroused as she moaned from multiple orgasms and now he was ready for the kill.

"Easy, big boy. I never get down on the first night."

Menna kissed Conteh passionately, tightening the grip on his now throbbing manhood.

"What the f...!"

"Language, Conteh. Do you always swear in the presence of ladies? I'm surprised at you. And living with your mum and four sisters too." There was a slight sarcasm in Menna's voice.

"Menna. You're not one of those fucking teasers are you?"

"No. I just don't fuck on the first night. Is that so hard to accept? Still, thanks for the pleasure. Not many guys know how to make a woman come without penetration.

Some guys seem to think it's in, out, shake it all about, and that's it. They don't realise that a woman needs more than that wham-bam stuff. I can see that you're my kind of man."

She got up and walked towards the kitchen. Nude. "I'll build a spliff," she added. "And don't tell me you don't indulge."

Menna had Conteh baffled. This was some woman. She had substance. Something different. She had it and he wanted it — badly. Perhaps it was the challenge of not conquering. Or her authoritarian attitude. Whatever it was, he would certainly come back for more.

Hours later, he kissed her goodbye. He settled himself into the soft white leather seat of his Beema, and checked his voice mail on his mobile. It was full. Marcia, Joya, Carmen, Collette and some he couldn't recall, wanted his body. He was still on heat as Menna had left him high and sticky. His balls were overflowing, and he had no intention of hammering the bishop. He had to score before the night was out.

It was 2am. Joya, Collette and Carmen were routine when it came to weekday nights. They had to work the next day and did not like their sleep disturbed. Marcia would be ready, so he dialled her number and headed for Solihull.

EIGHT

Simone was in a stinking mood when Conteh managed to drag himself downstairs. It was around 5am when he arrived home, and since he had a heavy night, he needed the sleep. Things had been pretty cool since their reunion, but now he was shitting himself. He wondered if she knew where he had been last night. Or even if she had caught another rumour of one of his escapades. All he knew was that if looks could kill he would be dead.

Simone looked at him long and hard and he became conscious of every inch of his body. Now he began to wonder if Marcia had left a dirty great love bite on his neck or something. She was one for trying that shit, only he was always cautious enough to stop her, but last night, or this morning, (since it was exactly 2:20am when he rang her doorbell), he had been a bit tipsy. He got even more carried away on her Cognac and, what with the earlier ital feast at Menna's, he could have failed to stop her eating his neck. Whatever it was, he wished Simone would spit it out. Fast.

"What's up, babes."

"Don't you fucking babes me, Conteh." Simone almost changed colour. Blood rushed to her face and anger settled behind her eyes.

She threw a single red earring at him and said, "Which tart did you bring into the house, you bastard! That cheap shit isn't mine! And don't tell me you've taken to wearing earrings now!"

She was more beautiful now she was angry.

"Simone. Baby. Keep your voice down. It's my sister's. Janet's." He had to think fast. "She lost it the last time she came. I forgot to tell you. When she rang to say she got home safely, she told me to tell you that if you find it, it was hers."

Conteh felt comfortable that his story couldn't be checked for the next six months. Janet was away in Jamaica on a long vacation. Without a phone.

"Look me in the eye, Conteh. Look me in the eye when you say that. Because as God is my judge, I'll never forgive you if you let another woman walk through my door!"

Tears flooded her face. Conteh held her close. As she sobbed he stressed his story and hoped to God that he got to Janet before she did. She had to save his salt fish. Big time.

Conteh wasn't blaming himself. He blamed Beverley's carelessness. Those were the earrings she wore when he dared to bring her back on that infamous night.

"How could you even think I would do a thing like that, babes?" lied Conteh. "I'm not that much of a dog. C'mon."

He was hugging her as he spoke and was pleased she wasn't looking in his eyes.

Simone walked to her drink cabinet. She poured a drink and slipped in a Diana Ross CD. This was all she needed on her day off — the thought of another woman under her roof. She sat down, curled up in the soft leather settee and stuck her head in Toni Morrison's 'The Bluest Eyes.'

Conteh sat down and cuddled up beside her. In trying to get her to relax, he stuck his hand down the front of her leggings and rubbed her stomach.

"Anything brewing yet, babes?"

"I'm trying to read my book. No, there isn't anything brewing. Don't you think I'd tell you if there was?"

"So don't you think we should try a bit harder?" He teased her neck with his tongue.

"Not now Conteh." Simone's lack of interest showed. "Time a' the month."

"Oh shit," he responded. He groped her breasts and kissed her mouth and said, "We've both been so busy, I forgot to mention that a friend of mine, Stanley, is having a party tonight. Wanna come?" He knew Simone didn't like going out when she had her monthly, and knew she would decline.

"Nah. I'll just relax tonight. But you go."

That was exactly what Conteh wanted to hear, since there was to be no party after all. He was taking Menna to The Blue Mango in Derby.

"Are you sure now, babes. I'd stay in with you but I promised Stanley faithfully."

"Conteh, I'm sure." Simone turned to her book again.

"I'll cook you a meal later. What d'you fancy?"

Guilt was talking. He didn't know why. Lying to his wife was nothing new.

"Why, what have you done?" Simone looked at him suspiciously.

"Very funny," he said and kissed her again, as he tried to overcome the ball of nerves that bubbled in his stomach.

Menna called her 'the Bitch,' for obvious reasons. It seemed she was being oppressed by her man, so in turn, she spent her spare time trying to oppress Menna, by mumbling verbal abuse laced with malice. They entered one ear, and went out the other. Menna had better things to do with her time and it was like water off a duck's back.

They used to be civil to each other. It all started when the Bitch dared to dip her mouth into Menna's business. She had tried to concern herself with a car that was parked outside the flats after she realised the owner was visiting Menna. The unwarranted concern was her problem. Menna couldn't give a damn. But when the Bitch took it upon herself to gossip to the neighbours about it, Menna decided to put her straight with a sharp tongue. Ever since then, the interfering blonde's claws were always out.

And her out-of-work photography boyfriend didn't help either. Did nothing but drove around with stalking eyes, peering from behind the tinted windows of his jeep, waiting to stick his prying lenses where it didn't concern him. 'Would do well working for the gutter press,' Menna thought. He would hang over your back fence to snoop at your dog shitting, if the price was right. And you wouldn't be too careful if you made sure your bedroom curtains were closed whenever you were undressing, or making love, or breathing, as you couldn't be too sure that his prying lenses weren't homing in on you.

At the outset, it was the Bitch who told Menna how snoopy he could get. He was paid to snap cheating husbands with their mistresses and visa versa. So there was no telling what the shinehead would do with his time.

When the Bitch's claws came out, one day it would be, 'Check out Miss Toffee Nose,' another time it would be 'She t'ink she nice.' The bottled-blonde thought she had arrived too, since she had mastered the art of patio with more fluency than a colonised parrot. But she broke the camel's back with: "Taken to stealing married men now have we?" She was a pot cussing an unsuspecting kettle. What she failed to tell Menna, was that she had whipped Garnet from his long-standing queen, Evadney.

Menna displayed her usual calm and collective disposition, leaving her antagonist wondering if she was deaf.

Was Conteh someone else's man? Was he really married? Perhaps she was stealing him without knowing. Perhaps the Bitch was right. There was no smoke without fire and the way things had been going, anything was possible. After all, it had been almost a year into the relationship, and she had not had the chance to lay upon his couch, use his shower, drink from his cups, or say hello to a single member of his family.

She thought perhaps the man himself could shed some light on the meaning of the remark, and a few days later, she asked Conteh to explain.

"Look, Menna, I thought you were intelligent enough to know not to listen to carry-go-bring-come! Can you see a ring on my finger?" He was like a cornered rat that had no choice but to attack. "If you want to find out if I'm married, call the Birmingham Registrar and they'll put you straight. Right now, I can't be doing with all this shit. If you feel better listening to other people and not me, then I don't think we should be together!"

They were sat in the bar at the Drum at the time, and Menna became conscious that his tone was drawing unwanted attention.

"Look, Conteh," she said in a low tone, "I'm sure that if the shoe was on the other foot you'd do the same. If you were told that I was married or was seeing someone else, you'd ask me about it, right? The thing is, I have good reasons for being suspicious. This relationship has been a bit one-sided wouldn't you say? I think it's sick that I could pass your sisters in the street, or even stand behind them in a shopping queue, or at a party, without them having the slightest clue that I'm sleeping with their brother."

"Look, Menna." Conteh's face showed a grave disapproval. "What's the rush. I told you, I'm not ready for all that introducing shit yet... Listen," he knocked back his drink, "I'll just drop you home. If you're not satisfied with how things are going, we'll just have to call it a day."

Menna was somewhat surprised at Conteh's reaction. She felt sorry she ever opened her mouth.

"Conteh, look... I'm sorry. It's just something the woman in the flat next door said. It was just bothering me and I had to say something. It's just a strange thing for someone to say without some sort of proof."

Menna followed Conteh outside. There was silence all the way to her flat.

"Listen, Menna, let's call it a day shall we." Conteh had left his engine running. "You're obviously not happy with the way things are going, and I'm not ready to take things any further right now. Yuh done know."

"Wait a minute. Are you dumping me?" Menna was perplexed.

"Menna... I mean it." He gripped his teeth and tightened his jaws. "I can't be doing with this."

'What have I done?' she asked herself inwardly. But she would not grovel.

"Okay. If you feel that way."

She made a speedy exit from his car, slamming the door with enough force to alert the whole neighbourhood, then she pulled it open again. "Fuck you, Conteh!" she added, now slamming it even harder (an action he hated), then headed for her own car.

She hit the road and before she knew it, she had underestimated the speed at which she was travelling. Flashing blue lights pulled her to her senses and seconds later, the voice of a police officer entered her head.

"Are you okay, miss?" The officer noticed her state of distress.

"No. I'm not."

"You haven't been drinking by any chance have you, miss?"

"No, officer. But I could do with a drink. Believe me." Menna managed a smiled. "I'm sorry. I was obviously speeding."

"Yes. You were doing 60 in a 30-limit zone. Look, I won't ask you to blow into a bag or anything. I can see you're not drunk. Personal problems?" He stood there like an understanding mentor, but staring at her breasts.

Menna looked at the officer and smiled. She was

grateful for his understanding.

"It is a personal problem, officer. But nothing I can't fix."

"You sure you don't want me to help you fix it?" he asked, still staring.

"If I change my mind, I know where to find you," Simone assured him. "And, officer, thanks for not booking me."

Menna did an illegal u-turn and headed for the comfort of her luxury apartment. Just then she could do with a girl talk, but it was rather late and her sister, Cynthia, would be sleeping. Angie, her close friend would welcome her calling anytime, but she was away in Jamaica with her man, Roy.

As she sipped a neat brandy, Menna looked at herself in the mirror and could see no trees growing in her face. She wondered how many other women found themselves questioning their physical appearance whenever men treated them like shit. How many of them have convinced themselves that they are not good enough? How many of them actually take the shit, until they have convinced themselves that they are just that? Shit.

She looked, and the mirror told her the truth. That she was still attractive, sexy and her figure was still in tact. Then she looked around her apartment and saw nothing but success. Framed proof of her achievements — school netball trophies, college certificates, diplomas, university graduation, her position as editor of *Black Star Magazine*.

"Why the fuck am I doing this to myself? Why do I let this bastard treat me like a piece of shit he's trying to wipe off his shoe with disdain? Who the fuck does he think he is anyway?"

Menna knocked back the remainder of her brandy then took a hot shower. It was late, but for her, the night was still young. Yes, she contemplated calling Conteh's mobile and telling him exactly what she thought of him, but she knew him enough to know that he would only listen to as much as he could take, then he'd cut her off. Like he's always said, 'You can't talk to an irate woman.'

Tevin Campbell was in the background and she didn't need that just then. Made her too blue. She ejected the heart-jerking CD and slipped in Gloria Gaynor's 'I Will Survive'. Somehow, it gave her strength. Now, every twist of her waist, every shimmy of her hips had a meaning. She felt as if she had stepped from a horrible era. 'I will survive!' she sang at the top of her voice, meaning every word of it. The reassuring song fought back the tears, and gently pierced a tiny hole in her ballooned heart, letting it down easy.

And she believed now, more than ever, that behind every strong woman, there was once a bastard man.

Menna filled her glass again and consulted her diary. The time didn't bother her. She dialled the mobile number of some guy she met at the Blue Mango in Derby just a month after she met Conteh. She promised she'd call but never did. She liked Conteh too much and had put Mr Blue Mango on the back burner.

Mr Blue Mango was certainly all that, with more than the average sex appeal, but just a little too full of himself. Of course, he would tell her that he was single and was keeping it down, waiting patiently for her call; that he had battled against the rush of testosterone and won — just for her. What the heck. She had nothing to lose. She wasn't about to do an out-of-the-frying-pan-into-the-fire act, but neither was she about to sit on her ass and mope. He was to be her stepping stone. A shelter in a time of storm.

"Menna... Hi... It's me." The voice on Menna's answerphone surprised her somewhat. It was tinged with a bad dose of remorse and grovelled intensively. It was Conteh. He wondered if he could take her out to dinner to make up for the way he behaved last night. It was the morning after the night before. He must have left the message in the dead of the night, for Menna didn't hear the telephone ring. Now the ball, it seemed, was in her court. She thought about it and decided that her strategy would be worth it. Along with the rest, she wouldn't call until it suited her. In fact, she wondered why she should ever call at all. For now, she'd let him stew. Besides, she had already planned to meet Mr. Blue Mango for a drink that night.

Simone climbed into bed with Mayo Angelou's *I Know Why The Caged Bird Sings*. The gripping novel had helped her to relax. Take her mind off a few things. She had been thinking a lot lately and questioned herself on several decisions she had made in the past, and wanted to make in the future.

It was peaceful. At that moment, Conteh was in a dancehall somewhere entertaining a large proportion of Birmingham's ravers, and she shuddered at the thought of what else he might be up to.

Her bookmark was a card, which held a telephone number. Lawrence's telephone number. She stared at the gold embossed figures and smiled, placing it at the side of her bed like a used teaspoon. A faithful used teaspoon.

Now she reflected on her encounter with Lawrence and felt like a naughty child that had taken a biscuit without permission. 'It was just a kiss,' she thought aloud. But she couldn't help wondering if he was making love to anyone at that moment.

She questioned her reasons for caring.

Conteh had been stewing for at least two weeks when Menna decided to let up. She could have stretched it for longer but her severed nose was spiting her space, big time. It wasn't easy for her. By no means. Still, it worked enough for her to be convinced that he cared more than she believed. This time, however, her eyes were wider. Out of bad came good and the situation had created a kind of cling-film for her heart.

She had enjoyed another exquisite meal at The Xaymaca Experience and now she lay between red silk sheets, listening to Conteh telling her how much he loved her. How he was sorry for acting the way he did. And how he didn't want to lose her. Earlier that day, too, she had had a visit from Interflora. A dozen red roses was accompanied by a note that read, *Only the best for the only woman in my life*. She was touched.

Menna realized then how much she loved him too, but still, she thought better of putting all her eggs in one basket. Of course she wouldn't sleep with Mr. Blue Mango, but would keep him as a form of security. He had taken her once for dinner and twice for quiet drinks over the past two weeks, and had impressed her, but not enough to turn her head like a fool. She knew full well he had the hots for her, but she was going to have it her way. It would be on her terms. If he didn't like it, he could walk.

Conteh was proclaiming his love for her, and it was blowing her mind, but she knew she would be no closer to even talking about seeing where he puts his head, or meeting his family. Everyone knows that a woman never feels secure in a relationship until she is introduced to her man's family, especially his mother and sisters.

Menna decided she wouldn't mention it again for a while. She would know when the time was right.

"Did you say it's been a year since we met?" Conteh asked. Menna was lying on her stomach. He laid his whole body on top of hers as if it was a shield. Her bed was cosy and warm from the heat they were both generating.

"Almost," she said kissing his fingers. Now would be the time to ask, 'Well now you're back, what's gonna change?' It was all too easy to slip back into the same old routine, like a newly located piece of jigsaw.

"Time flies," Conteh replied.

"Yes. But everything else seems to stand still as far as we're concerned." She had forgotten her promise to herself.

"Menna." He dragged his voice seductively. "Don't spoil a beautiful moment. Please." He teased her neck, kissed her face and ran his tongue down the whole length of her spine. She felt like a queen.

"Okay. Okay." She had half-expected another eruption.

"Listen. I know how you feel about this 'meeting the family' thing. Just give me another six months will you, babes. T'ings will get better, you'll see. If they don't, I give you permission to dump me. Feh real."

Procrastination is the thief of time, and Conteh needed no lessons in procrastinating.

"What do you need another six months for? Don't we already know each other long enough?"

"Babes we just had a bust-up. You need time yourself. What if I drag you home to meet my mum now, then a week later you have a relapse?" He kissed her firm black nipples between words.

"I think you're speaking for yourself, but let's not go into that," Menna agreed, feeling rather horny.

They engaged again in another session of passion and Menna was reminded again of why she loved him so. Conteh even tended to the parts of her body she herself had no interest in. He kissed her from the sole of her feet, to the top of her head. Touched her in places she had forgotten existed. Mastered her body like he owned it. He made her feel important. Wanted. Loved. Foreplay was heavenly. She was climbing the walls, and it took some wicked will power to resist, as Conteh was about to enter her — without a condom!

"Conteh." She reached under her pillow and produced a rubber sheath.

"Oh, fuck." Conteh came down a gear or two and rolled onto his back. "Are you fucking HIV positive or something? Or perhaps you think I am?"

"Look I'm not going there again. We've already talked about this." She sat up. "If you don't want to make love with a condom, we don't make love at all. Listen. When you walk through this door tonight, I won't know where you go. You tell me you live with your mother and four sisters. Fine. But I don't know that. The only way I know to reach you is by a mobile phone. Failing that, I can always turn up at your shop. Where do you suppose we'd make love if you couldn't come to my place? In your car? Or in some seedy hotel room? Still, I chose to take this shit because of the way I feel about you. This relationship has been too one-sided for you to expect me to put my life in your hands. I'm not saying you're HIV positive. What I'm saying is, 'I don't know'. As a matter of fact, you don't know either, because you haven't had a test. I know I'm not, because I've taken the test. And I intend to keep it that way. Negative."

Conteh stared at Menna all through her poignant speech. Of course he had heard it all before. Not least from his dear wife.

"Okay, babes. I hear yah. Jee-zus." Conteh got up and walked nude to the bathroom. The mention of the big A had taken his appetite clean away.

The sound of a running shower told Menna he was going, without making love to her. She lay there staring up at her own reflection in the mirrored ceiling.

"You going then?" she asked when he re-entered the room, still drying himself.

"Yeah, babes. I've got a few things to do before I open

the shop tomorrow. Besides, I've got to pass 'round the studio to see how the guys are doing with the recording."

It wasn't long before he was dressed and the last bit of sound from his engine left her ears.

She looked over at the clock. It was just past 1am. She wasn't sleepy and felt inspired. She walked nude to her living room. She poured herself a Martini and lemonade, walked over to her PC and opened her file on Single Black Female. Words came easy whenever she was hurt, upset or even angry for whatever reason. Now they flowed from her mind like water from a tap.

Simone settled into position, her body dovetailing with the contours of her husband's. Conteh's arms were wrapped around her. She spoke with a comforting calm in her voice.

"Conteh, how pleased I was when you told me you would take the AIDS test. At least we know now that we're both negative. It is down to you to keep it that way. If we are trying for a baby we must be sure that we will be around long enough to see him or her grow up, and that the baby is healthy too." Simone stroked her husband's chest as she spoke.

Conteh held her close, and kissed her forehead in reply. But as they laid there between red silk sheets in readiness for the giving and receiving of sexual pleasure, he began to trip again on guilt. Joya, Collette, Carmen, Marcia and Menna troubled him and, secondly, he had developed too deep a feeling for Menna. Though he hated to compare, there was a similarity to when he met Simone. Now he recalled one of his mother's old sayings: 'If you bite off more than you can chew, you will choke.'

He didn't know it yet, but Conteh was choking all right.

"Conteh, what's the matter? You seem so distant." Simone noticed her husband's absent-mindedness.

"Oh, I'm cool, babes. Just a few problems with the sound. Nothing I can't sort." He kissed her face and told her he was tired. He didn't need to say it, for it was blatantly clear that he wasn't horny. Simone knew her husband had to be seriously worried about something to refuse sex. She kissed him and said good night.

The next evening found Conteh and Nico conversing over their pints at Faiths, their favourite Hagley Road haunt. This was where the men would chill, away from anything that was hardcore, including music and women. When it was warranted, new hopefuls (in the female sense) would be taken to Faiths too.

"This is serious shit, Nico. I think I'm madly in love with Menna. I can't even believe it's over a year now since I've met the woman. Time really flies, man."

"It tek yuh a year to fall in love wid dat niceness, star? I would have fallen from day one. She's hot. I only saw her from behind. But if the face goes with the ass I saw leaving your shop that day, say no more." Nico boiled everything down to sex. He took nothing serious, even when his mate wanted him to. "That's probably why you won't let me meet her. Frighten I might tek her weh?"

"Nah, man. It's not just her looks." Conteh ignored Nico's last sentence. "There's more to her. She's got something over me, man. Can't put my finger on it though.

Got her head screwed on as well. She's different from the other bitches I messed with in the past, man. On top of that, she wants to talk serious."

"Fuck!" Nico nearly choked on a mouthful of Bud. "Tread easy, star. The wife, man. Shit. You don't want t'ings getting out of control."

"Tell me about it. I told her I wanted to call it a day a few weeks ago. Just to play things down a bit. You know. So she would get off my case a bit, ease the pressure an' all dat. She was pretty upset. We made up now. But I don't want to lose her, man. It's greedy, I know, — but... I would give up all the others for her, man. Just like that. Except the wife of course."

"You've got it bad man. Real bad." Nico now saw the seriousness of the situation. He knew his mate well enough to know how much he was sizzling for Menna. And when it goes past just the hots, then care needed to be taken. "You're in trouble, star. Anyway, I still wanna know how come I haven't met her yet. Shit. Nearly a year? Yuh definitely frighten' I might tek her weh, man. Dat's it," Nico chuckled.

"In time, man. In time."

Conteh took the last sip of his drink and asked Nico if he was ready to move.

"Yeah, man," Nico responded. "Got to get the flat ready. Got this hot chick coming round tonight at midnight. Jade. You're not the only one who can pull them, ya know, star. Dis one hot, nuh raasclaat."

He was his usual uncouth self.

Conteh wasn't interested. He had problems of his own.

NINE

"Home an' dry! Home an' dry!" Conteh's voice echoed the triumph of the night. Vibes Injection had scraped the floor with Magnum, a rival sound system that was competing against them for a gleaming trophy. As the speaker boxes pushed out a 'special' from Luciano, singing Vibes Injection's praises, the room echoed a thunderous roar of approval. Big bumpa bashment girls moved in slackness style with their gold toothed shaven headed boyfriends. Dreads, funky-dreds and baldheads alike, the vibes were level.

Like a host of programmed robots, the crowd obeyed Conteh's request to 'Flick up unnuh lighters, and 'Hands in de air.' But pandemonium broke out when Senseh Fowl fell against one of the enormous speaker boxes — blood, spliff, bullet and all. Now the crowd moved only to one tune — the tune of emergency exit, if they were lucky enough to find one.

A throng of bodies piled against each other as they tried desperately to find the one and only door to their safety. Lives were almost lost in the rush, as numerous fallen ravers were trampled on under panicking feet.

White ambulance men and police officers looked out of place amidst the sea of on-looking black brethren and sistren who came out to be drenched in music, but were now drenched in the blood of panic, and a mike MC.

The bullet, that nearly did its intended job, had lodged itself somewhere around the vicinity of Senseh's brain. It was triggered by a follower of the rival sound who didn't appreciate being flopped. As Martin Glynn said in his poem 'De Ratchet A Talk':

De ambulance man a' tek weh de victim
De policeman a' tek weh de criminal
But dat deh night, inna de scuffle an' de fight
De guilty one escape
Yes de guilty one escape.

Tonight, it was a gun that had escaped into the hands of another bredrin, who had pulled its trigger, putting yet another cloud over people's passion to fill their brains, hearts and souls with strong reggae music.

Senseh survived the ordeal of the bullet, but a wheelchair now replaced his 5 series BMW. If he could talk, he'd tell you, he'd rather be dead.

Conteh and his sound crew were gutted at the loss of their boy. A cooling off period followed the tragedy. After rethinking the whole situation, Skankie and Rankin' Zukie, two long-term members of the crew, chose to give up the sound game and spend more time with their families, rather than several hours behind speaker boxes at a dance where love could switch to hate and out your lights in the blink of an eye. *Feh real.*

"That could have been me," said Conteh as he watched the pitiful helplessness of his idrin in his wheelchair, for he had been standing where Senseh was standing only moments before.

The vacation was well needed by Conteh to take his mind off the shooting incident. It was hard to come to terms with Senseh's misfortune and Simone didn't object to him cooling out. She had no more leave left and couldn't go with him. So he closed up shop for a few weeks, and packed his bags and took that well needed flight to Jamaica.

His sister Janet met his flight at Kingston International.

"Whaap'n, sis? Looking well."

Janet could see through her brother's forced smile.

"Sorry to hear about Senseh."

"Me more than you, sis." Conteh hugged his sister and followed her to a waiting taxi. His intention wasn't to hang with relatives this time. It was strictly for relaxing. Of course he would visit, but his hotel room was waiting, and Marcia would be keeping it cosy until he got there. After all, she paid for the whole shebang. She would make her own way to the hotel, as the slightest clue to the fact that she was with Conteh would freak Janet out.

Conteh knew that throughout the holiday, he wouldn't have to put his hand in his pocket much. He would wallow in Marcia's generosity. But he knew she was looking for a good return on her investment.

Of late, Marcia had been very demanding. He had cooled down drastically on how much time he spent with Joya, Carmen and Collette because of Marcia. They had left umpteen messages on his mobile, none of which he returned. There were a few threats of kiss-and-telling to the CSA, but he had been down that road before and had long since come to the conclusion that all he needed to do was to 'pass 'round' and cool their tempers, the way only he knew best. Then there was Menna…

"I know you don't need this now, Conteh, but we need to talk. I want more than this."

Marcia stared at the blue horizon, as slight waves splashed her feet simultaneously. Her head was laid across Conteh's chest as they lay on a beach in Negril. "I know how we started, how I said I wanted things, but as I told you before, things have changed. I'm too much in love with you to have it any other way."

Conteh sat up, perturbed.

"Look, Marcia, I thought we came to JA to relax. Besides, you know what you want is out of the question. I love Simone. And I won't leave her. You can't say I've ever told you anything less. I can't just drop her now because you have decided to change your mind about our little arrangement. T'ings nuh run so a raasclaat."

He was angry, but so was she.

"So you still see me as just a fuck, eh?"

"Isn't that what you saw _me_ as to start with, Marcia? A good fuck."

Conteh looked deep into her eyes. He knew he didn't love her, but couldn't say he didn't care somewhat for her. If the relationship came to an end, he'd miss her money more than he would miss her. Men have needs. Different needs. Sexual, financial, domestic — and a few that go even deeper. And if they can't get them all from the woman they call their own, then, without a doubt, they will seek them elsewhere. It is one of the harsh realities of life that is so hard to swallow. It is best left at the back of one's mind.

"Fuck you, Conteh! Fuck you!" Marcia stormed off towards their hotel.

Conteh watched her hurrying up the beach, then moved towards a palm tree and lay in its shade. He told himself he'd leave her to cool off. Something he always did when his women blazed up like wild fires.

A local woman walked by with her hands on her hips and a basket of mangoes on her head.

"She lef' yuh t'raas," she shouted, emitting a mocking belly laugh.

Conteh woke an hour later, sun drunk. If he had been a white man, a lobster would have nothing on him. When he got back to his hotel room, a strange feeling overcame him. He walked out again to check the number on the door. Then he checked the wardrobe, and found only his clothes hanging there. Marcia, it seemed, had checked out. Luckily, she left his passport. It was laying on the bed next to a note that read, *Nobody uses me, you bastard! You're gonna pay.*

He knew he had rattled her cage, big time, and that she would definitely rock his boat, yet he stopped wondering where she was and turned his concern on himself.

"You were here with a woman!"

Janet wasn't going easy on him. She knew her brother was no angel, but she liked Simone and it felt like she was deceiving her too.

At the top of her voice, she called him a dog when he

asked her to lie about the earring Simone had found in
their bathroom.

"Conteh, what the hell is wrong with you? Aren't you
ever gonna stop screwing around? You've got a lovely
wife. You won't find anyone as good as her again, and if
you don't watch it you're gonna lose her. For good this
time. Mum done tell yuh dat a'ready. I can't lie for you. I'm
a woman and I wouldn't like it. Bringing some slut into her
house? And coming to Jamaica with a woman other than
your wife? God, you…" Janet was lost for words.

"Calm down. All you're saying is true. All that's behind
me now. Trus' me. This will be the last of it. I love Simone.
Just do me this one favour. If she asks you when you get
back. Please. Please. Say the earring is yours, sis." Short of
getting on his knees, Conteh couldn't appear more sincere.

Janet paused for a moment. If that was needed to save
his marriage, how could she refuse?

"Are you sure you won't be seeing this Marcia gyal
again? Or take another woman into the house while
Simone is away?" she quizzed him.

"C'mon, sis. Marcia left me stranded. Bitch. She took
my fucking ticket for crissake. And all my dollars. I have to
call Nico so he can wire me some cash down. Does that
sound like someone I'd want to see again?"

Janet stared at her brother like he was dirt.

"And, no, I won't be taking anyone to the house again."
He looked away with shame.

Janet sucked her teeth and cut her eyes. "I don't agree
with it, bro'. It's disrespectful. Yuh mek yuh bed, Conteh,
so I should mek yuh lie in it." Her disgust could not be

mistaken.

He looked at her. "Bwoy, yuh soun' jus' like mum."

Back in Birmingham, Conteh was recovering from jetlag when Simone walked into the lounge. His snoring startled her since he hadn't called to say he would be back from Jamaica so soon.

"Conteh?" He stirred. "I thought you were staying in JA for two weeks?" Simone was leaning over her man, looking concerned.

He could have stayed the whole two weeks. Nico had wired him enough money, but he was too troubled about the note Marcia had left in the hotel room. It made him uneasy about her next move. He had seen that *Fatal Attraction* shit.

"I missed you, babes. I had to come back. Give us a kiss."

They hugged each other. Conteh closed his eyes again.

"It's a good thing I wasn't up to no-good. You know. Like sneaking someone in knowing that you are miles across the sea," Simone joked.

Conteh got jittery. He opened one eye to look at her. He wondered if she had found out about how the mysterious earring had got behind the loo seat after-all, and was testing his reaction with irony.

'You may think I'm fine when you leave...' Marcia sang, trying to match the dulcet tones of Macy Gray. It was midnight. A lavender candle burned at the head of her bed. '...But I'm just a prisoner... of your love...'

Now tears came with the words and she sobbed like a neglected child.

Then came the twisted temperament. Her long red nails raged war upon her bedsheets to the sound of ripping silk. Marcia had bought the set because Conteh said red silk sheets turned him on.

'So good. So fucking good.' Marcia echoed his words, only this time the words described the sound of destruction.

Now she was strong again. Like sun after rain. Strong and hungry. Hungry for revenge.

Marcia swung her ass into the Golden Touch as if she owned the place.

"D'you mind doing the banking now, please, Candice?" Conteh said to his assistant when he felt the angry gust of Marcia's presence.

Candice took the hint and make herself scarce.

"Marcia. What's happening, babes?" Conteh felt somewhat uneasy. It was their first encounter since she left him stranded in Jamaica. He hoped she had found herself another dick thing.

Marcia's face was within kissing distance of Conteh's. "I want my twenty grand back. That's what's happening. Will two weeks be okay for you?"

Conteh eased back. "Marcia. Are you crazy?" His smile was stiff. "You said yourself it wasn't a loan."

"No such thing as a free lunch fuck-face." There was evil in Marcia's voice. Conteh knew he was in trouble.

"How the fuck am I supposed to come up with twenty

g's in two weeks? Business isn't all that good, y'know."

"Sell your dick." To Conteh's surprise, the avenging lady grabbed his balls and squeezed. Hard. "It's the only asset you've got of any value right now." She eased a long red nail gently, yet nastily, down the side of his face. "By the way, your wife is beautiful."

Conteh grimaced. The colour went from his face. How did she get to see Simone? Had she found out where he lived? All he knew was that he didn't want her anywhere near his wife.

"Listen, Marcia, if you go anywhere near Simone..."

"You'll kill me?" she laughed like a mad woman. "Like I said, two weeks." She grabbed his chin, like he was a naughty child and planted a bitter kiss on his lips.

Hours after Marcia's visit, Conteh still felt like a piece of shit. He thought of how he could have landed one on her when she was all up in his face, couldn't understand why he didn't. The only thing that he had been able to think of as he watched Marcia's long legs leaving his shop, was to 'out her fucking lights.'

But something was making him uneasy. Earlier, while Marcia had his balls in her hand, he could have sworn someone was watching. Someone who made a speedy exit before they could be seen. He hoped it was his imagination. *Feh real.*

"Nico." Conteh sounded like a drowning man and Nico could tell straight away that something was seriously wrong.

"What's up, star?"

"It's that bitch, man. Come inna de shop wid one bag of bumboclaat threats."

"Who, Menna?"

"Nah, man. Marcia."

"You what? What kinda threats?"

"Said she wanted her twenty grand back in two weeks t'raas! Not just that, but I think the bitch got my home number and my address. "

"Raasclaat!" Nico was stunned. "This is serious shit, blood. I thought that love shit with Menna was serious, but now you've got real problems. There's only one way to deal with stupid bitches like that, star. Box up her bumboclaat."

"And what good will that do me, Nico? I have to think logically now, man. Yuh nuh 'ear weh me seh? De woman 'ave me address, home number, every t'ing to rahtid... Listen, I'll link yuh, later. Around seven. Mek sure you're in, bredrin. Me haffi talk to yuh. Serious."

Nico was pleased he didn't arrange to see Jade that night. She still hadn't met his best mate. That was how she wanted it and it was fine by him. She was a strong woman. The type you listen to.

Conteh knocked back the large measure of Jamaican rum Nico had poured him. Straight. It went down the hatch as smoothly as a glass of his mum's carrot juice. He was mad, and his bloodshot eyes showed how much.

"Are you sure this is what you want, Conteh?" Nico asked, as he built a huge spliff.

"It's either that or lose my wife, man. Marcia isn't going

to fuck me up so easy. She was the one with all that 'No ties, no commitment shit. Now that she lost control, fell in love and want more, she's trying to turn my fucking life upside down. Bitch! It ain't gonna happen, Nico. No way."

"Yuh sure yuh don't want to sleep on dis one, star? Is dis t'inking logically? You know t'ings cool wid me. I can fix dat, no problem. But you just have to be sure. You can't get more final than that solution."

"I'm sure, man. Out her fucking lights."

Nico had a worried look on his face. When Conteh had given him five grand out of his 'loan' from Marcia, he had happily taken the money and bought himself a new motor. But outing her lights was another matter.

Conteh took the spliff Nico handed him and pulled vengefully, inhaling enough ital to last him through a famine. He stood up and walked restlessly around the living room like an expectant father. "The sooner the better," he added. "Before she comes back with that dyam facety attitude. Or even approach my wife. Who the fuck does she think she is anyway, Nico? Gyal a' flex like she mentally sick."

Conteh was high. It had been a long time since he had been so high. The closest he'd come to contemplating anything like this was when some pussy bwoy, (one Janet called her boyfriend), made the mistake of laying his hand on his sister. The bwoy had lived to regret it. Closer still was when one of his sound followers, high on crack, held a knife to his throat and threatened to duss him out. Conteh wouldn't let him into the dance and the dopehead didn't take too kindly to that. A few days later Nico saw to it that the crackhead was done over in a dark alley. One infamous Bongo Dee put in an appearance and made sure that, along with a crucial beating, this knucklehead lost his razor touch. He severed the thumb and index finger of his right hand — the two fingers that gave support to that impertinent knife. *Feh real.*

So when he finally left Nico's flat that night, Conteh knew that everything would be everything.

When he got back to his house that night, he was pleased that Simone wasn't home. He was too high and too troubled to face her. She was on a flight to Tenerife and had left him a note.

Thought you'd be home before I left for my flight. Your mobile was not switched on. Please leave a message on mine to let me know if everything is okay. See you tomorrow. Miss you. XX.

Conteh felt guilty. He looked up at the portrait of his wife and regretted ever hurting her. Ever deceiving her. He dialled her mobile from their landline telephone and reached her mailbox. 'Simone, sorry I missed you, babes. Stopped off at Nico's. Can't wait to see you tomorrow. Love yuh bad."

He needed a shower and headed upstairs.

It was carnival time again. The weather was faithful. The sun was beating down on stalls, heads, bare backs and uncovered asses. There were floats from Bristol, London, Manchester, Cardiff and every city that was worth a mention.

Carnival queens flaunted their bodies and outfits like proud peacocks, and steel band members beat their drums and gyrated their hips like chicks in a Jamaican yard. Everyone who was anyone could be seen somewhere in the thick crowd. Lamberts, Philberts, and Desmonds walked innocently with their main women, glancing and winking at Patsys, Jacquelines and Sonias, women who were stealing their love on the side.

Conteh twiddled with the knobs on his deck and was pleased to see the faithful crowd that gathered around his sound system. He felt like Jesus with his disciples.

"A'right?" he asked when Joya walked by, deliberately flashing her new hair style, her trim waistline and her firm ass in front of his face. She didn't stop. She was walking with some Joe Grine who thought he had arrived now that he was holding on to one of Conteh Egyptian's women. Joya smiled a *touché* smile at Conteh. Conteh smiled at her naivety. Man an' man knew the word on the streets and what Joya didn't know, was that he knew that her Joe Grine was checking a blonde t'ing in Balsall Heath. 'A nuh not'n.'

Carmen and Collette came by too. Had to let him know that they were around. Carmen had her hair weaved and she had it going on too. She made damn sure of that. She wanted to entice. Collette was natural, her hair cut short.

"A weh de raas me a' see yah!"

Conteh's eyes nearly popped out of his head when two Marcias walked towards him, looking as if they had just stepped out of *Vogue*. The other woman had to be Marcia's sister.

"You're not doing them as well are you, Egyptian?" Skankie, a member of the sound crew was gasping at the sight of the two women. "Bwoy. How yuh do it, man?"

Marcia was now in Conteh's face.

"How's it going, lover boy? I knew I'd find you here twiddling your knobs."

"Marcia. Ease the pressure, nuh. Cha?" Conteh forced a smile to give Skankie the impression that Marcia was rushing him for his dick.

"I'll ease the pressure as soon as you come up with the goods, babes."

Marcia gave him an attitude look and walked on, taking her 'twin' with her.

"Bwoy, Egyptian, are you on a ginseng diet or somet'ing, man? Whatever you're on, me want some a' dat. Trus' me. Yuh is definitely de girl's dem luck, t'raas."

Conteh kissed his teeth and carried on twiddling with his equaliser buttons. At the same time he tried to take in the main show as the floats went by with old men (reminiscing over baa-ba-boom times) grabbing their crotches and moving their middle sections as if they had ants loose in their pants. Policemen walking amidst the happy crowd, forced smiles when Lilt-ladies lookalikes grabbed them unexpectedly and wheel and turned them to the merry-making music. Every man, woman and child looked criss. Like they had all gone out specially to buy the outfits they wore, just to walk down the streets of Handsworth on Carnival day.

Necks were filled with gold. Chaperitas hung from wrists. Tommy Hilfiger, Nike, Calvin Klein, Fila and Reebok gear were worn to impress. The poor looked rich. The sad looked happy. Everyone looked as if 't'ings did a gwaan fi dem.' Vibes were level and everything seemed like everything.

A man in his twenties, wearing a black Kangol hat, dared to drive his Beema through the impossible crowd. He steered with his left hand and hung his right elbow over the driver's door as if it was about to fall off — Jamaican taxi driver style. He tooted as if he thought the crowd would part, making way for him like Moses and the Red Sea..

"Dat's de trouble wid black people. Too dyam extra," a larger than life woman with an original African style backside showed her annoyance, and cut her eyes at the forceful driver.

"Jus' move yuh bumboclaat outta de way!" The driver had no respect for her sex, or the fact that she could be his mother. All he wanted was to get where he was going.

"Who yuh t'ink yuh talkin' to?" she responded, walking over to his car.

"Yuh want a box, woman?" The driver went darker with anger.

The heated exchange between the Beema driver and the fat lady were now the centre of attraction in that section of the merry-making. Two boys in blue attempted to make their way to the scene, but the crowd was too thick. Before they could get there, the fat lady rammed a right hook into the driver's face and dented the side of his car with her left foot. The fat lady hurried from the scene laughing a real belly laugh, and saying "You raas, yuh. Don't fuck wid me, bwoy! Yuh must know yuh place!" Her friend followed with praise for her.

"Bongo Dee? Raas! Yuh cyaan mek no woman duss yuh so, man. Yuh should floor dat bumboclaat!" A man in the back of the Beema spoke.

"Your car shouldn't be here, sir." A policeman was looking down at an angry Bongo Dee. He could hardly hear himself speak, as the car shook with the heaviest bass line.

"Cool, officer. Cool. De driver is not well." It wouldn't do to say that a female had t'umped him up good and proper, since egoistic pride was at stake. The man in the back made his way to the front. He was clad in a bad bwoy suit and his neck was weighed down with enough gold to start a jewellery business.

"Ease over, Bongo. I'll drive."

He gripped the wheels with fingers adorned with 24-carat gold knuckledusters. He grimaced at the officer, displaying an oversized gold crown. The officer moved them on.

Bongo Dee was fuming as he held his bruised face and glared upon his dented ride. Blood poured onto his white designer shirt from the teeth that went flying with the blow. He didn't know which was worst, his tilted pride or the sight of his car. "Dat woman dead, bwoy!" he spoke for the first time. "She dead, me a tell yuh. No raasclaat woman fuck wid I an' walk free. Nat even my madda!"

"T'raas," his friend echoed an endorsement, housing his right hand in the pocket of his suit and dragging on his freshly lit spliff. He handed the slender concoction to Bongo, who needed it like breath.

"Whaap'n, Bongo?" Nico had caught the tail end of

what had just taken place. He touched fists with Bongo Dee. He was eating a plate of curry goat and rice and trying hard to avoid it soiling his white bad bwoy suit, trimmed with gold, and the white Fila loafers that kicked it off so well.

Of course Nico didn't take Conteh's desire to 'out' Marcia's lights seriously. He was no murderer. Neither of them were. Conteh was just expressing his venom in the heat of the moment. A few days later Nico confirmed that Marcia was safe and well. All they had done was warn her to stay away from their boy. To calm herself down. To seek psychiatric attention. Everything was clean cut. Sorted.

A cold shiver ran through Conteh's body when he realised what a heated moment could do. He thanked his lucky stars Nico lacked the same temperament as Bongo Dee. Things might have been different. He buried his head in the here and now. As far as he was concerned, the whole Marcia episode was dead and buried. At least he hoped it was. He didn't want that thorn in his side again.

TEN

Cynthia had dropped by unexpectedly. She hated to see her sister being taken for a ride, so when Menna told her she was cooking Conteh a special meal, she thought she would use her nose, like a pig, to pry. After all, it had been too long now, and still this Mr Vibes Injection was still undercover. A figment of everyone's imagination, as far as Menna's family was concerned. He didn't show for their cousin's christening. He didn't show for Christmas. He didn't show for a family wedding and, most of all, their mother's 60th. All to which he was invited. The speculation was, he didn't show because he didn't want to be shown. His sound was always playing. When it wasn't his sound, he had to be in the studio, overseeing the putting together of crucial tracks. Or he was doing some promotion somewhere and had to tend to the formalities.

"Hi! I was just passing. Something smells nice," Cynthia's voice boomed as she stuck her head around the kitchen door, then proceeded to where her protagonist was cooling out.

Cynthia had met Conteh once before. Now he was meant to be tuning her sister's piano. What she knew of him was not good. Cynthia knew of Joya, Carmen and Collette. Menna also knew all about his baby mothers. As he was always reminding her, he had to 'see his children.' Menna was down with that. If there was one thing she loathed, it was men who multiplied but didn't provide. But what she wouldn't be down with, was the fact that he still hung his trousers in the wardrobes of these baby mothers, and warmed their beds for a few hours, from time to time.

Menna followed her sister into the living room, to do the formal introductions, before returning to the kitchen to finish the cooking.

"You mean, you can't remember me?" Cynthia asked.

Conteh looked at her hard. She did look familiar. He had seen so many faces in his dances, cooed at, stopped his car and leered at, one-slammed so many, she could be anyone.

"Do I know you?" he asked.

The music was down low. Aretha Franklin was doing her thing.

"Short memory." Cynthia made herself comfortable on the shagpile carpet in front of the stereo, like it was her yard.

"How's Joya these days? God, I haven't seen her for ages. She's got a son for you, hasn't she? Or is it a daughter? Does she still live on...? What's the name of that road again?" Cynthia was bluffing. She hadn't seen Joya since they played netball umpteen years ago. And as for knowing where she lived now...

Conteh's memory kicked in. The jigsaw fitted. Cynthia Jarrett.

"She was okay the last time I went to see my son." Conteh squeezed the words reluctantly from his throat, he didn't want to engage in dialogue with her.

"And Collette?"

Now she was pushing her luck.

"What's this? Twenty questions?" Conteh knitted his brows and smirked at the same time. Cynthia was under his skin. "I'm not their keeper, you know. They've got my children, that's all." He fiddled with the dials on his mobile as if he had suddenly remembered to make a call. It was always close by. Like a string of worry beads.

Cynthia sensed his uneasiness. Birmingham was big, yet small at the same time. A man could have a woman in Balsall Heath, Kings Heath, Smethwick, Spark Hill, Edgbaston and Moseley at the same time, and none of these women would ever meet, let alone have a clue that the others existed.

"Don't get touchy. I'm only enquiring about old friends."

Conteh wished he could shut her a box. 'T'ump out her bloodclaat teet'.' He was wondering how familiar Cynthia really was with his baby mothers — although, baby wasn't the operative word. His youngest children, two sons and one daughter were nine, ten and eleven years old. His older children (the ones he knew of) were sixteen and over, and he didn't see them so much now that their mothers had new partners and would not let him have his cake and eat it.

At least Cynthia didn't know of his marriage. If she did, that would be the knife she would use to stab his life out, only too happy to furnish her sister with the knowledge. That was a relief at least, but he was still bothered about the idea that she might be familiar with his baby mothers.

'You know how women chatty-chatty,' he thought. 'Like chicken in a yard, to bumboclaat.' Had to kill the bull before it killed him. He had come to Menna to cool out. Chill. Take his mind off the Marcia thing. But he didn't get the chance to. Instead, all he got was a raas nosy sister, sticking her nose in where it didn't belong.

He would do anything to save his own ass. He called it survival. And today, he was going to survive even if it meant hurting Menna again.

"This is lovely, babes."

Conteh was leaning over a plate of Menna's Chicken Montego Bay. Cynthia had left and they were now alone. She had cut her eyes at Conteh, gave Menna the 'I would kick this one to the kerb if I were you' line and left, swinging her behind like a straw brush in a dirt yard.

The candle-lit table was like a picture out of a romantic novel. Marvin Gaye serenaded them with some 'Sexual Healing'.

"Thank you."

Menna poured wine into a fine pair of crystal glasses. The same ones she had poured sangria into last Valentine's day. She had bought them especially for the occasion. She remembered the glint in his eyes as they had toasted 'to the future,' a single red rose between them. And she was happy.

"I wish things could be different between us, you know Menna. You done know." Conteh sipped his wine.

His mobile rang but he didn't answer it. Instead, he switched it off.

"What d'you mean, Conteh? I'm getting used to the

relationship the way it is. Don't start wishing anything now. It's okay. Come to think of it, there's no big deal with anyone meeting anyone's family anyway. It doesn't mean much really. I could meet your family today, but you could still be screwing around."

Conteh looked up at her suspiciously. Did Menna know more than she was letting on? It was times like this that he despised intelligent women.

"I hear yah, babes. But you won't think so when you hear what I've got to say." He fiddled with his fork.

"Don't tell me. You want to call it a day again," Menna jumped to her own conclusion.

"No. It's just that something unexpected has come up. It's just that…"

"Just that what, Conteh?"

He eased his chair back as if to distance himself from any missiles. "Before I met you, I had a very close friend. There was nothing sexual between us." Menna glared and listened. "Over the past two months we've been seeing each other. Not on a sexual level though. Just friends." Menna knew what was coming and got up as if to find some strength to endure it. "Anyway, we just realised that we both have deeper feelings for each other and…" He pushed his luck to a dangerous limit and his plate further away from him.

"You mean you want to fuck her? Or are you doing so already?" Menna was livid.

"Is that all you can say, babes?" Conteh was lacking words.

"Look." He had started, so he'd finish. "This chick is

easy-going. She's not into all this meeting the family shit."
His tone was demeaning. "I know you've changed your
tune now, but before when I told you I wasn't ready, you
weren't too pleased. And although you said you're getting
used to things the way they are, I know it won't be long
before the subject will come up again. Still, I can't blame
you for wanting commitment, babes. But like I said, I'm
not ready for all that yet."

Menna's appetite flew right out the window along with
her self-esteem. She glanced at the flame from the burning
candle and knew that she would always hate its glow now.
That it would lay in her subconscious forever. Not as
romantic, but as something nasty. She lit a cigarette. She
only smoked on moments like this. And she hadn't had
many.

She stood now with attitude. One hand held her
cigarette, the other on her hip. She waited. Waited for the
moment that Conteh would tell her more about this chick.
The one she saw all up in his face, with his balls in her
hand, when she passed by his shop. When her heart had
stopped pounding and she could think straight, she
decided to hold it and watch the ride. She couldn't explain
how she did it, but she held it down. Waiting, watching,
planning. She had told no one. Not Cynthia. Not Angie.

"So, who is this unlucky chick then, lover boy." Conteh
hated that 'lover boy' label. It reminded him of Marcia. He
remembered that she too called him lover boy.

"You don't know her. She's a blonde." He was as cold
as ice. He had detached himself from his emotions and did
it like a job that simply had to be done.

Menna choked on her cigarette. Conteh's reply took her way off the beaten track and swung her across the thin line between sanity and insanity. She grabbed one of the crystal glasses and aimed for his head. It missed and smashed on her freshly painted walls. The result expressed the state of her life. A mess. Before she could gather her thoughts, Conteh had already started his engine. He had made a speedy exit.

Menna would never forget the smell of burning silk. Burning red silk. Silk so romantic, now tainted with hate.

'How could he be so cold?' Menna asked herself.

Conteh pulled up outside his house and chilled for a while before going inside. He leaned back against the soft leather interior of his luxury Beema and lowered the sound on his stereo. Sanchez spoke to him through a heavy bass line, like he was sharing his feelings yet again.

Conteh was messed up. He wanted out of the game, but in order to unravel the tangled web of deceit he had woven for so long, he had to hurt some people. Ruthlessly. Like a soldier on a battlefield.

The blonde bombshell didn't exist. He had watched *Waiting to Exhale* with Menna, and remembered how she empathised with Angela Basset when she was dumped for a white woman. He knew it wouldn't go down well.

The next day, Menna spent her lunch hour with Angie.

Angie flicked her blonde hair as she listened to her pal. She herself had been taking shit from Roy, her 2Pac lookalike boyfriend. The women had spent countless hours sharing past experiences. They needed no one to tell them that a woman was a woman — black, white, Asian, Chinese. Whatever creed or colour she may be. And that men are bastards in the same capacity when they break the hearts, and mess up the minds of their women. Period. Hearts and minds are colourless.

"I suppose he thought he was twisting the knife in when he told me he was dumping me for a white woman." Menna sipped her liquid lunch as Angie listened, flicking her hair and blowing puffs of smoke periodically. "He had seen my reaction to such a scene in *Waiting to Exhale* when we watched it together," she continued. And d'you remember that Karen episode? I told him all about that too, girl. So he knew."

Yes. Angie could remember the Karen episode all too well. Karen was Menna's friend, though not exactly 'bosom' buddies. The two women were introduced when Karen was looking for someone to pick up her son after school. At the time, Menna had time on her hands and didn't mind doing it. Karen had time on her hands too, but wanted to use it for 'more important things'. Like sitting under a sun bed for hours, keeping her hair groomed, her nails manicured and her make-up flawless. She could afford to. She was sleeping with an Italian who was married, rich and paid for the air she breathed. All he wanted in return was for her to lay her body down anytime he showed up.

Over the years, Menna and Karen became close. Menna was there for her through thick and thin. Even when an American she had met led her up a Madison Garden path.

Karen had bought a wedding dress, acquired something old, something new, something borrowed, and sold the contents of her house and was planning her trip to America, to what she thought would be a wedding in paradise. Her world came crashing down like a ton of bricks when the only contact she had for Mr America (a telephone number aboard a ship), went dead. So was her heart. Her final acquisition — 'something blue.'

Again, Menna was there to prop her up. Gave her a shoulder to cry on and opened her ears, heart and mind to her well-needed chats. Menna had been there with shitty men and knew full well that it could happen to anyone. She stuck around even when Karen's so-called long term friends found her situation to be no more than the latest gossip.

And Menna's faithfulness didn't end there either. When she found out, too, that this glamorous lady who lived on nothing but her good looks, had messed up at school and now had the literacy skills of a four year old, she set to teaching her the basics in Maths and English.

"I can't believe a nice, attractive woman like you hasn't got a man," Karen had said to Menna one day. As if not having a man was like having the plague. "I know someone. He's really nice. I'll introduce you."

Menna laughed. She wasn't desperate, but she agreed to play the game.

Days later, a hunk turned up on Menna's doorstep. He and Menna hit it off straight away and they started dating. A year later, he announced that he was leaving her. For Karen. Period.

Karen stayed undercover for days. When Menna finally reached her by telephone, she poured salt into her wound by cussing Menna for not being able to give the man what he needed.

The following day a policewoman, accompanied by a male colleague, was sitting in Menna's living room, reminding her of some Act or the other that could work against her if she left anymore threatening messages on Karen's answerphone. She had acted irrationally when the twisting knife connected with her bones, and the salt had sunk deep into her wound.

Menna had not set eyes on Karen since. The last she heard was that the relationship with Mr Boyfriend ended with a black eye, which stood out so vividly, even when Karen tried her hardest to cover it up with a mop of blonde hair.

Menna did not condone women beaters, but she would have lied if she had said she didn't gloat for at least a week as Karen was hoisted by her own petard. *Feh real.*

"Angie, I told the man everything," Menna continued. "So I suppose he thought he knew what would do my head in. But shit, a pussy is a pussy — black or white. And a black woman who puts up with shit isn't any different from a white woman who does. Conteh is the one who is a heartless bastard."

Angie wished she could share whatever Menna was feeling emotionally. After all, she had been there for her when she was sixteen years old and had packed her bags to leave her parent's home. She had fallen pregnant for Roy, and was more or less told that she had let the family down. Especially when there were so many nice white boys she could have. It was Menna's mother who took her in, until she found a flat of her own.

"Typical. He tells you all this *after* he's eaten your meal. You would have thought he would spared you the trouble of cooking for him." Angie was looking at the sheer selfishness of the man. "And to think how he wooed you with all that sweet talk and flowers after that night at The Drum. Practically begged you!"

Conteh wasn't in church today because he wanted to be saved. Far from it. Gladys' church was having a mini concert and she had invited him. It wasn't as easy as that though. Conteh came up with all the excuses he could find, as to why he could not attend. He finally gave in when his mother made him feel as guilty as hell. She reminded him of when he used to be such a loyal servant of God. How the brethren and sistren used to love him so. When his Bible was a permanent fixture under his arm. And how he was now doing the devil's work in the dancehalls, playing the devil's music, yet found it so hard to spend a few hours in the house of the Lord.

"Mum, it's a Saturday. You know I play out on Saturday nights. I have to be there to make sure that everyt'ing run smooth. This is a sound clash spectacular."

"I cyan't believe you have become so ungodly, Conteh. When the Father comes we'll see if you're goin' to tell 'im dat you're not in his number because your soun' clash spectakilla was more important than his house."

"A'right, mum. I'll come. Jeezus!"

"And don't call the Lord's name in vain."

"It's not in vain, mum. I need his help to endure your nagging," Conteh joked and hugged his mum.

Gladys smiled. "Janet and Sandra are coming. They might 'ave left the church but they still remember God."

"And I don't, mum?"

"I don't know how you cyan remember God when yuh runnin' aroun' wid all dem women when yuh 'ave yuh wife. Yuh need prayer!"

"Mum. Don't go there, man."

" 'Mum, don't go there?' 'Mum don't go there?' A' tell yuh over an' over again. Yuh too much like yuh faada in dat way. Dat girl is goin' to leave yuh. Den we'll all see where you're going to get dis love chile yuh keep talkin' about."

Conteh sighed and picked up a banana from his mother's fruit bowl. "I'm going, mum. See you Saturday," he announced.

He couldn't stand the heat and he was getting out of the kitchen. Fast.

The little church was heaving with bodies. All the seats were taken and visitors stood in crunched bunches anywhere they could find. Mothers hushed their young babies. Young children, who didn't yet understand the meaning of tact, strained their necks and fixed their eyes on the faces of people they hadn't seen before. Ladies wore their dresses with pride as they tried to outshine each other. The selection of hats were enough to make a day at Ascot seem ordinary.

Nothing had changed, thought Conteh. Nothing, except for him.

Conteh's Auntie Gertie smiled at him from a rostrum seat. She stood out from the crowd like a mango amongst seedless grapes. She wore a pretty-pretty frock, a proud straw hat and fanned herself frantically with a fan embroidered with red and yellow flowers, a busy humming bird on one side and a map of Jamaica on the other. Later she would hug Conteh and say, "Lord, what a way yuh handsome. Jus' like yuh faada."

The concert was in full swing. Thelma bellowed "Just a closer walk with God," and made the whole church spring to its feet, glorying, *amen*ing and *hallelujah*ing. She almost moved something in Conteh too, until he remembered that not so long ago he had seen her in a club in Bristol. Vibes Injection was playing there at the time and he nearly dropped his end of the speaker box he was carrying when a second glance confirmed it was Thelma. She was clinging like velcro to Federal G, a mike MC who was sampling her chow-chow at the time. "Don't tell me yuh backslide," Conteh had said then, as soon as he got the chance to talk to her.

Thelma giggled nervously and asked him to keep his mouth shut. Real tight.

After the collection plates had overflown, Pastor Brown took his stand on the pulpit. He was on a mission to gather lost sheep to the flock, and Conteh was sure he was talking to him and him alone.

"Weary wanderer," he shouted, and the congregation echoed a wider acclamation. "The Lord is waiting with open arms."

"Amen!" Sister Golding lifted her right arm and gave a speeded-up version of the Queen's wave, then shook as if someone had suddenly dropped an ice cube down her back.

"Fornicators!" Pastor Brown jumped on one leg and did a circular turn, banging the pew like a judge.

Conteh felt a surge of heat. He looked up and caught Sister Brown's eyes. He wanted to get up and leave, but the row he was sitting in was so tightly packed, it wasn't worth the contemplation. Besides, he would have disturbed too many sacred knees to get by. He looked the other way and realized that Janet was looking his way. She winked at him and he knew that she knew how he felt.

"Yes, I said fornicators! Sneaking around like thieves in the night! Deceiving! Lying! Taking your vows for jokes! The Loooooord is watching you!"

Simone gave her husband a serious look and looked away again.

"The day of reckoning is comin'!"

"Shalamashalamashalama!" Sister Harrison stood up quickly, did a spin and sat back down again, sucking in air, like the after effects of accidentally eating cayenne pepper.

"You lied in the face of the Lord! I will forsake all others — you said! And cling only to my wife — you said!"

Conteh was now positive that someone had taken his name to Pastor Brown. His left leg shook and he kept his eyes on the floor, where there were no condemning eyes.

"Repent! In the name of Jeeesus! Confess! Right your wrong!"

A possessed woman raced from the back of the church and threw herself in front of the altar. She must have hurt herself. Sister Mcqueen danced on one leg towards her and tried to hold her down. It wasn't easy, so brother Festus went to the rescue. The woman wailed as if a member of her family had died, and when Pastor Brown spread the five fingers of his right hand across her head and shook hard, she fell flat on the floor as if something had suddenly let her loose.

Now the whole church was on spiritual fire.

Deacon Ellis held his head down and was praying hard.

"That's her," Sandra whispered in Conteh's right ear.

He hadn't realized his sister was sitting behind him, funky dreads and all. They were longer now, and the cute rectangular-rimmed glasses she wore made her look like a sophisticated rasta woman.

"That's who?" Conteh turned discreetly towards his sister.

"The woman Deacon Ellis is meant to be knocking off."

"You what!" Conteh's whisper came out louder than he expected. Perhaps Pastor Brown was not talking about him after all, but about Deacon Ellis.

"Came out in confession I heard," Sandra said.

Deacon Ellis always had that Godly look about him. A look Conteh could remember ever since he had sense. He couldn't begin to imagine the possibility of him doing the nasty with a woman other than his wife. There had to be some mistake. Later, in the back of the church, Conteh looked over at Sister Ellis, who was now serving the curry goat. She didn't seem troubled. She was still emitting that haughty belly laugh she always had. Then he looked at the woman who damned near killed herself at the altar. The one Deacon Ellis was meant to be fornicating with. Sister Ellis was now piling curry onto her rice, and they didn't seem to be generating any hostility towards each other. In fact, they smiled at each other. Conteh knew this was church, but surely church people got jealous too. There had to be some mistake.

Somehow, he couldn't imagine Simone being that civilised with Menna, Marcia, or any of his baby mothers.

Thelma tapped him on his shoulder.

"Whaap'n sexy?"

Thelma blushed at Conteh's presumptuousness. She wouldn't have minded him being so bright in a dance hall, or even on the street, but this was the 'house of the Lord'. Besides, her mum was standing only a few feet away from her.

"Did you enjoy the session in Bristol?" he asked.

Thelma cringed and scolded Conteh with her eyes.

"Did you come to the convention in Bristol, Conteh?" asked Sister Golding. "How come I didn't see you?" She had overheard Conteh's question and was sure that the session he was asking her daughter about was one of a spiritual nature, and not one of a ragga flava. She would have had a fit if she knew that her spotless daughter regularly visited a 'house of hell' as she would call it.

"Yeah, yeah Sista Golding. Wasn't it good?" Lying became him.

"It was glorious. And how are you, Conteh?"

"Surviving, Sista Golding, surviving."

"You looking well." She smiled, shook Conteh's right shoulder and walked away.

Conteh did the sign of the cross and breathed a sigh of relief.

"Talk about close, Conteh." Thelma sighed too.

"Who you trying to kid anyway, Thelma? You know you can't keep this two-faced thing up forever. Bit hypocritical wouldn't you say? It's either the dancehall or the church, man."

"Shut up, Conteh." She looked around to check for listening ears. Who are you lecturing?"

"Me? Lecture? Is one t'ing me waan do right now. Me waan fi oil up yuh cyan." He lowered his voice and leered at Thelma's ass.

"You'll never change, Conteh. Have some respect will you? And to think, your wife is just over there."

Conteh looked over at his wife. She was happily chatting away to his mother and two sisters. Of course, he loved her, but he wouldn't say no if Thelma had obliged.

It hadn't taken him long to forget Pastor Brown's words about fornication.

ELEVEN

Menna laid heavily on Conteh's mind. Cutting and
running wasn't that easy. He was seriously in love with
her. He had tried desperately to contact her, but in vain,
and now withdrawal symptoms were seriously setting in.
He waited for her to call him after he had dropped the
blonde bombshell, waited for her to beg him to give her
another chance, but she didn't. He figured he would give
her some more time.

There he was, in love with two women and five women
(that he knew of) in love with him. Although only Simone
and Menna mattered to him to any degree, (since Joya,
Carmen and Collette all knew where it was at), it didn't
make things any easier.

It was nearly two months after his little blonde story
and he still couldn't get hold of Menna. Everyone else was
on his case, but no sign of her. He wanted her back and
would do whatever it took. He knew it wouldn't be easy,
but a drowning man will clutch at a straw.

Conteh pulled up behind Menna's sports car but was
somewhat reluctant about knocking on her door. After all,
he had called the shots so things could run to suit him, so
he could only blame himself if it had backfired.

Menna would have no problem finding a man. In fact,
men would find her. The thought of another man making

love to her, twisted his stomach up.

After the fourth ring on her doorbell and a few minutes wait, Conteh decided to give up. He pulled away from her place and headed for Nico's flat to roll a spliff or two, sink a few Special Brews and catch up on what's been going down.

Nico was home all right, but unlucky for Conteh he was entertaining. He answered the door in nothing but a pair of silk boxer shorts. His eyes were sleepy with sex and his body radiated happiness.

"Looks like you're busy bredrin."

"Yeah, man. Jade." Nico lowered his voice. "Hot, nuh raas. Tell you, man. Think I could get serious wid dis one, star." He chuckled. " 'Body like silk — sof' an' smooth'." He imitated the voice of Shaggy, for the benefit of his idrin.

"Wha'? Is weh yah seh? Did Nico Kaur say serious? Raas. A' betta let yuh get back to her, man. Feh real."

"Did you pass by for anything special?" Nico asked.

"Nah, man. I was just cruising. Too much on my mind, man... Needed a spar's shoulder to lean on..."

Nico looked towards the bedroom. Jade was waiting there and he was beginning to feel rude. Besides, he knew she would tell him how rude he was. It was like turning down the grill on sizzling bacon.

"Listen, rude bwoy, I know what you need. You need cheering up. Remember that foursome idea I told you about? I'll fix it, man. It'll do you good. Trus' me."

"Well, it certainly won't hurt. Catch yuh later, star."

"Respec'."

Nico touched fist with Conteh then closed the door.

When he returned to the bedroom, Jade was pulling on the spliff he had left burning in an ashtray by the bed.

"Who was that?" she enquired.

"Me idrin, Conteh. But less about him. Where were we?"

Nico dimmed the light even lower and Jade lifted the quilt and let him under. He took the spliff from her fingers and pulled hard on it, as if to recharge his batteries.

"Is this Conteh as nice as you?" Jade teased.

"Don' matter if he is. He's married. I told you, he runs a jewellery business in town, and a sound." Nico paused. "Anyway, why am I talking about my mate when I'm supposed to be making love to my woman?" Nico placed the spliff on the ashtray, slapped Jade's ass playfully and they romped like a pair of puppies, simmering into more serious business.

"I still don't know why you're being so secretive with me you know, babes," Nico said when their passion had subsided. Why won't you tell me where you live? Why I still can't come to your house? Why the mystery? You know how much I check for you. I have never taken this shit from anyone, so you must know that I really care. How long you want me to be patient for?"

The bachelor of the century was after commitment?!

"There's no mystery at all, Nico. I'm just not ready yet. You're just not used to it. Don't tell me you haven't done the same to women in the past?"

Nico knew she was right but he still couldn't comprehend. Women just didn't do this kinda thing.

Nico decided to stop bursting his brains about it, and

concentrate on loving her. For the first time, he had found someone he really felt something for. He was madly in love with her. She said she loved him too, so he had to accept that all she wanted was time.

Joya and Carmen seemed to have taken the hint that he wanted to cool things, although Collette had called to say that she was pregnant, but she wasn't going to keep it, as she was thinking of doing a BA in Sociology. Under the circumstances, Conteh didn't give a damn. He had other important things to do, like saving his marriage and getting Menna back.

"Cheers, star," said Conteh, hitting the edge of Nico's glass with his own.

"Feh real," responded Nico.

A miniature bottle of Wray & Nephew rum stood empty on the coffee table and a 750ml bottle of Daniel Finzi Reggae Spiced Rum was fast becoming history. The men had already sunk several cans of Special Brews and were now in high spirits. Practice had made them perfect and they could hold their liquor like Mike Tyson could take punches. Fingers were busy building spliffs and the video recorder was poised for the showing of a blue movie.

The two men were getting ready for a cosy party for four. The long awaited orgy Nico had promised to fix was finally about to materialise. In less than half an hour, a blonde and a brunette would be attending the rendezvous at Nico's exquisite bachelor's pad. Not that they needed any help, but the high volume of booze and the weed of wisdom were helping them to relax, and would strip them of any inhibitions they might have had. They were nasty all right, but having an orgy was a first for both of them.

Sanchez, Dennis Brown, Chaka Demus & Pliers, and Diana King sparked up the air. Bobby Brown was 'humping around' when the doorbell rang. Nico checked his teeth in a nearby mirror, squirted a whirl of breath freshener in his mouth and obliged.

"Hi, Nico!" The blonde sounded excited. The brunette followed her in with a smile. The girls knew what they were there for, and left their airs and graces on the doorstep and the bottoms of their skirts at home.

"Go straight in, ladies. Meet Conteh."

Conteh looked up and nearly choked on his drink. The blonde was certainly no stranger to him. He had done the dirty on her in the past and didn't think he'd see her again, at least not under these circumstances. He was one of the bastards Sharon told Nico about when they first met. After a year and six months of seeing Conteh on a purely one-sided relationship, she found out that he was married. He had several more fish to fry and didn't bat an eyelid when she told him to take a running jump. He simply kissed his teeth and drove off. This was the first time he had seen her since the confrontation and he couldn't believe his eyes.

"Well, well, well. If it's isn't Mr. Heart Breaker himself." Sharon's surprise seemed a little fake.

"Sharon! Shit! What's happening, babes?" Conteh chuckled nervously.

"I see you're still up to no good. Unless you're now divorced of course." Sharon did her usual flicking of the hair stuff.

"I see you two know each other." Nico was puzzled. Then he recalled his conversation with Sharon on their first encounter at Scotties, and did his own reckoning.

"I wish I could say I'm pleased to see you, Conteh, but I'm not. Still, I'm no party pooper." Sharon was flippant beyond Conteh's comprehension. This was a woman so cut up the last time they were together, he wondered how he had escaped her wrath.

"So what are you doing with yourself, babes?"

Conteh tried to change the subject.

"I work for a magazine. And when I'm not doing that, I do what you do best, Conteh. Using men for sex."

"I don't use men for sex, Sharon. Whatever I am, I'm certainly not gay."

"Very funny." Sharon sat on the floor and made herself comfortable. It was almost as if she'd been there before. "By the way, this is Melissa," she added, gesturing towards her bubbly friend.

Conteh reached forward, took Melissa's hand and kissed it. Bright. "I'm sure it's gonna be a pleasure knowing you, Melissa."

"Likewise." She wasn't shy.

Nico handed both ladies a drink and placed an ashtray on the floor in front of them, a large spliff sticking out of its side.

"Who said we need to get high to screw you guys?" Melissa showed how relaxed she was.

"I'm sure you don't. You should do this for a living girls," said Conteh half-jokingly. "That way you'll be having fun and getting paid for it." He reflected now on

Maggie, his teacher in love. The woman who took him to heaven between red silk sheets.

"That's not a bad idea. Tell you what, Conteh," Melissa lounged towards the sofa where Conteh was sitting. "As you've come up with such a brilliant idea, I'll do you for free."

Too right, she didn't need any intoxication for raw fornication. She grabbed the waist of his jeans and began to undo the catch.

"Go, girl!" Sharon egged her mate on.

Conteh didn't object and lifted his ass high to make the task of removing his jeans easier. Nico and Sharon had started a party of their own too. That wasn't the Sharon Conteh had known. She was a totally different woman from the one that was now using his best mate's dick as a lollipop.

As Conteh enjoyed what Melissa was doing to him, he couldn't help thinking that he helped to make Sharon what she had become. A first class tart.

'I like the way, you move that thing.' Sisqo's 'Thong Song' filled the air.

It wasn't long before the cosy little party had turned into a real steamy orgy. The Reggae Spiced rum, Wray Nephew and the drags of marijuana seemed to have taken control, and the night took on a blueness that would have them both shocked the next morning.

The mood of the room became any which way, and while Melissa choked happily on Conteh's dick, she enjoyed the vigorous movements of Nico's manhood inside her. He moulded her hard pink nipples as she accommodated him from behind, while Sharon devoured Conteh's mouth and licked his body all over.

Conteh's mind flashed to his wife, and a surge of guilt pulled him from his rude disposition. He froze for a moment and it showed.

"Lighten up, Conteh," Sharon coaxed him. She could feel his hesitancy.

"Can we open some windows or something? Let some air in this damn room." Sharon spoke with purpose. Authority. She rose assertively from her knees and walked over to the nearby window. "There we are," she said, after opening the curtains and extending the lever on the window. She stood there for a few seconds, looking out onto the darkness as if she was waiting for something. Sprinkles of rain raced in through the open window and cooled her hot, red face.

Conteh must have lightened up like Sharon had told him to, for now he had joined her at the window. He embraced her back with his chest, coupled her breast with his hot palms and nibbled her ears.

She smiled mischievously out into the darkness. Then she turned towards Conteh and picked up where she left off. Nico's double glazing was strong enough for the force of their bodies. Simultaneous flashes of light entered the room, illuminating their dirty deeds.

Soon the four bodies were a muddled heap on Nico's shagpile carpet again, swapping, touching, eating, entering. The heat of the night generated ecstatic moans as the four bodies climaxed simultaneously.

The curtains were still open and the window ajar, and

Conteh could have sworn it was flashes from a camera. But when the humid night ended in a torrential downpour and fiercer flashes of lightning, he was convinced that it was paranoia in action.

Conteh and Nico died and went to heaven. They were both shagged out and had nothing left to give. Lifeless, they fell into a coma-like slumber.

Dawn broke to find the two men naked, lifeless and with thumping heads. Their guests had left, satisfied and smiling, pulling the door closed behind them.

"That was some heavy shit, man." As Conteh spoke, a serious fear overcame him. The booze and drugs had left his head, and for some reason he recalled the talks he had had with Simone and Menna about safe sex. The lecture he promised to heed. He remembered the fun of last night and how sweet it was. He remembered entering two promiscuous women without any protection at all. He thought of his wife again, but quickly dismissed her, for now he couldn't stand the guilt.

Conteh held his head and began to gather his clothes. In the cold light of day, it wasn't a pretty sight to see him and his idrin totally nude, in the presence of each other. Besides, it could give the wrong impression if anyone happened to knock just then.

As Conteh retrieved his underwear from a corner of the living room, he noticed a shiny diamond and sapphire ring on Nico's mantlepiece. It was familiar. Too familiar.

He picked it up, puzzled. It was the very same ring that Menna had bought from him. The one he had engraved with his own hands.

"Nico. What's this ring doing 'ere, star? This is Menna's. You haven't been doing my girl have yuh??"

"Egyptian. Talk sense bredrin. Not'n nuh go so. Yuh know me don't deal wid dem t'ings deh." Nico was puzzled. "Menna's ring?" he continued, "*Your* Menna's ring?" He homed in on the exquisite piece of jewellery. "That's Jade's ring, man. She must have dropped it there the last time she was around."

The plot was now as thick as the ground in an open pig's pen on a rainy day.

"Nah, man. This is definitely Menna's ring. Wait a minute..." A strange thought entered Conteh's head, and his face was a question mark. "This Jade... have you got a picture of her?"

"Nah." Nico secured the fastener on his Armani jeans and walked over to close the window. "But I have a video. Of us doing the nasty."

"Get the video out quick, rude bwoy. You kinky bastard, you," joked Conteh.

But it was no joke.

It wasn't long before the two men were tripping on the naughty home video, and Conteh almost wet his underwear when he recognised that sexy ass.

Jade was Menna! Menna was Jade!

"A weh de raas, Nico, dat is Menna, man!"

"Are you sure? Look good, man, it could never be."

"Nico. Is the pope Roman? Dat is Menna. Believe me."

Nico was baffled. "It all ties up now... " He held his spliff like an important stage prop needed for his lines.

"Wait a minute. Yuh not telling me Menna was in your

bed the other night when me pass round?"

"Yeah, man. Shit. We even talked about you. Fuck, I told her that you were married. I know how you tried to keep that shit from her. How was I supposed to know she was Menna?"

Conteh's mind was now working overtime. 'What was Menna playing at?' Birmingham was filled with crazy women. Why was she seeing Nico under disguise and a different fucking name! The mystery was beyond them both.

"She knew what she was doing, man. Give the bitch her due, she's fucking clever. I can't believe this. The only woman I could ever admit that I love, t'raas." Nico was choked.

"Yeah, man. She knew what she was doing. She knew we knew each other. Trust me. The bitch!" Conteh was piqued. They both were. Outsmarted by a woman. The shoe was on the other foot and it didn't feel nice. They didn't like it one bit. They didn't have the right to be angry, but nevertheless, they were. Big time.

Sharing Pam, Sharon and Melissa had no effect on the men, but somehow, they didn't like the fact that they had shared Menna — Jade, whoever. She was special and they had both fallen in love.

Both men spent days talking to Menna's answering machine, knocking her door, leaving irate, cussing notes and even lying in wait for her. Her gleaming Mercedes Sports had now disappeared, and she was nowhere to be found. She was lying low. They tried desperately to link her, but without success. Conteh even turned up at the offices of _Black Star,_ only to be told she no longer worked there.

Time was longer than rope, and she would have to show sometime, the two men figured.

Trouble again, and it was all too much for Conteh.

A man, around forty, entered the Golden Touch with vengeance in his eyes, fury in his fists and a gleaming blade under his jacket. It was most certainly not good for business.

Conteh had never seen this brother before, but was anxious to know who the hell he was. He didn't know if it was the right thing to do, but he kindly asked the two customers who were browsing at his jewellery counter to leave. The angry man had already hinted that he wanted it so. The customers could see that something was up and did so obligingly. Conteh turned the closed sign outwards, and turned to face the Mike Tyson lookalike who was now swelling like a balloon, and breathing like a bull.

"I hear yuh 'ave some young daughters, mate?" There was obviously a reason behind the angry man's question.

"Yeah? Get to thee point, mate." Conteh could do without this.

"How would you like it if I breed-up one a' dem?" The man didn't wait for a reply. Instead he puckered his lips, lunged forward and grabbed Conteh by his neck. Seconds later, a heavy fist greeted Conteh's left cheek, and the side of his display cabinet caught his falling head. When the man brandished a gleaming blade, Conteh saw the gates of hell.

"Woah! Woah! Just a minute, bredrin!" Conteh spluttered, concentrating on the blade that was too close for comfort to his neck. "What's the problem, man?"

"My sixteen year old step-daughter Cerise, that's the problem! The one you took advantage of in your car nine months ago. The baby was born three days ago. I thought it was someone her age, man. Not someone old enough to be her father. When she told us, I swore I'd kill you! 'Egyptian,' she seh. 'Conteh Egyptian?' her madda asked. 'Yes,' she seh. Her madda faint straight away."

Conteh tried to ignore the pain in his head and reflected back on Cerise, the pretty young thing he took advantage of in the back of his Beema a while back. He remembered her girlish voice, yet womanly body. He remembered her screams as he robbed her of her innocence. He could see her face so clearly now and said, "I didn't know she was under age, man. Believe me."

"The law will deal wid yuh, man. Lef' it to me, you'd be dead!" The man shoved Conteh against the wall and the knife nicked his neck, then he left the shop, still in a state of fury. Conteh gathered himself and thanked God for the air he breathed just then.

He dialled Nico's mobile only to find he had some problems of his own. The tape in the video used to film the lecherous foursome was missing. 'Where the fuck could that be?' he wondered.

"Conteh! What happened to you?" asked Simone the following morning when she noticed her husband's missing front tooth and his grazed neck.

"Some idiot tried to snatch a gold watch from the shop yesterday. I tackled him and, in the struggle, I fell against the wooden edge of the cabinet. Knocked me dyam tooth out to rock stone. I have to go to the dentist tomorrow to sort something out." Through practice, Conteh had become a perpetual liar, and the trumped-up explanation came easy.

"Did you manage to hold him until the police came?"

"Nah. I didn't get a chance to call the police. The bastard slipped through my fingers like a flash. Still, the main thing is, he didn't get the watch."

Conteh wished she would quit quizzing him now.

"You should still call the police. Is that security camera of yours sorted yet?"

"Nah. Just my luck too. I must get it looked at next week. Let's not talk about it anymore, babes. I'll just put it down to experience."

Simone got the message and picked up her flight bag. She wasn't looking forward to her flight to Palma, but duty called and she had to go.

"See you later, darling," she said, kissing her husband's forehead.

"Don't work too hard, babes," he said as she descended the stairs.

As Simone closed the door behind her, she couldn't help but puzzle over Conteh's blasé attitude over the attempted robbery.

Conteh struggled to recognise the voice at the end of his mobile. The woman spoke with a familiar tone, but he still couldn't place her. It wasn't unusual for strange women to obtain his mobile number from flyers and tickets printed to promote his dances. They would call him pretending they wanted more information when, in fact, the crazy bitches were after a piece of Mr. Vibes Injection.

"Who is this?" he enquired, still shook up from the event the day before.

"How easy you forget, Mista Entertainer," The lady sounded perturbed.

"How easy I forget…? It's Mitzi, isn't it? Nah, it's Carol."

"Look. I'll probably be here all day if you're gonna call names. Let's cut the crap. We need to talk. Where can you meet me?" The lady was assertive.

"Hold on a minute." Conteh sat up from his relaxed position. "I get an irate stranger on the end of my line, saying, 'Where can you meet me?' and she's expecting me to agree to a rendezvous."

"Yuh dyam right." She was even more irate.

"What if I'm in danger?" asked Conteh.

"You're always in danger, Conteh. The life you lead. Listen. This evening. 7 o'clock in the bar at The Matrix Art Centre. I'll recognise you."

"Who are you?"

"Be there." The lady evaded his last question. Before he could speak, she clicked off.

"What the f…!"

1471 was no good. The mystery caller had made sure of that. He dialled Nico again. "Listen, bredrin, jus' had a weird one. Some woman want me fi meet ar at de Matrix tonight at seven. After yesterday, I'm not willing to meet anyone on me own, mate. Man, woman or pickney t'rahtid. But I feel I should go."

"I'll be there, mate," Nico assured him. "In the background though. Seven o'clock, yeah?"

"Yeah, man. Later, star." Conteh clicked off then chucked his mobile across the bed. He spent the rest of the day trying to backtrack on all the women he'd tangled with lately. The ones who had been a quick flash in the pan, one night stands, etc. He had eliminated all young girls from his guesses. His mystery caller sounded too mature and assertive. He couldn't figure out who it could be, and decided to leave it all to the mercy of later on.

Conteh hated the feeling as he walked towards the bar in the Matrix. Whoever she was had the advantage. She was probably watching him as he walked.

He looked to his left and saw a wickedly attractive black woman about thirty, walking towards him in a red Nike T-shirt and jeans.

"I see you made it before me," she said. "Actually, I sat in my car for a while. By the way, you don't need your sidekick. I'm not armed and dangerous. Well, perhaps I should say, I haven't got a metal shooter, and I won't physically hurt you." She had recognised Nico at the opposite end of the bar. "Shall we sit over there?" She pointed to a small table in the corner.

Conteh stared curiously at the raving beauty and was still puzzled as to who the hell she could be. Whoever she was, she had claimed the right to seize the handle, so, for now, he must prepare to hold the blade. Conteh was nervous. As the stranger fumbled in her large handbag, he looked over at Nico, his face filled with curiosity.

"I must have changed a hell of a lot. I must admit, I was much plumper then. Plumper and, I suppose, stupid. Jacqueline. Jacqueline Smith. We met at the Scratcher's Yard years ago. Funny how history repeats itself isn't it?"

Conteh's memory was well and truly jogged. But he could see her now, in her youth. Feel her too. The slow dance, the boyish chat-up line. Well before he met Maggie, his teacher in love. One of his many conquests before he knew what lovemaking was all about.

"Jacqueline! Shit! It's been at least… seventeen years?!"

"I see you've learned to count, Conteh," she sneered.

"So… Why all mystery, baby?"

"I'm not your baby." The correction was abrupt. "For your information, I brought your baby up single-handed until she was ten. Then I met and married her stepfather Henley. He treated her like his own. She was doing so well. Her grades were so good. But she's changed."

Blood rushed to Conteh's face. "What are you telling me, Jacqueline? That we have a daughter?"

"Ten out of ten for hitting the nail on the head, Conteh."

"But I thought…"

"You thought I killed her? Got rid of her like you said? Slept well for all those years, did you? Thinking I'd killed our child?"

"Jacqueline. Keep your voice down. I didn't know. Feh real."

"You didn't know, Conteh, because you thought I

would be heartless enough to walk down to the suction shop. And what would you have done if you had known? Ignored it like all the others you knew about? Anyway, that is not the real reason why I'm here." She dragged on her cigarette.

"Yeah?" Conteh was even more intrigued.

"Cerise. The girl you got pregnant...? She's your daughter, you scumbag." She spoke through clenched teeth now.

"What the fuck," Conteh stood up and sat back down again quickly, like a disturbed jack in the box. "Jacqueline.. He paused to catch his breath. "Tell me dis is a rahtid dream. Please."

"Believe me, I wish it was. 'Conteh Egyptian' she said. I actually fainted. I nearly died. My husband wanted to kill you. If he knew the whole truth he probably would have."

Conteh sat holding his head. "I can't believe this. Nah, man. Nah. Nah." He looked at Jacqueline. "So what do you want me to do? What can I do? If I had known it was my own fucking daughter... Shit." He felt like a heap of hog-infested mud. "Things can't get any worse for me, man."

Violins were needed.

"I suppose I am partly to blame," Jacqueline shared the problem. "I should have at least told Cerise. It would certainly not have come to this. I just didn't want her to have anything to do with you after you told me to kill her. I was only young then but do you know how I felt?" Tears welled in her eyes.

Conteh became uneasy. They were already attracting attention.

"Why did you decide to tell me?" Conteh had to know.

"So you can share the torture, Conteh. If you've got any conscience that is. If I'm to be punished by guilt, knowing that because of me, my daughter gave birth to her own brother, your son/grandchild — whatever — then you have to bear that cross too. If it weren't for this, you wouldn't have heard from me. Ever."

"Right. Okay. I see. Well, it's working already. I feel punished. Trus' me... Listen, you've got my number. The child and Cerise will be catered for. Just try and stop this police business, will you? Look, Jacqueline, I'm... sorry."

He held his head at the temple as the reality of the whole situation hit him like a ton of bricks. He couldn't turn the clock back. The whole world would see the shame written all over his face. "Listen, babes, call me from time to time. We're in this thing together. Feh real."

He recalled his mother's philosophy on the madness of sleeping around recklessly. She often told him of a man in Jamaica who was so free and easy with his love, that he ended up fathering so many children and he lost track. As a consequence, some of his offspring grew up to give each other that all so forbidden love.

He felt a cold shiver. It felt like he was dead, and that someone had pissed over his grave. He recalled his numerous rendezvous with girls young enough to be his daughters, and remembered how many times in his deeper past he had disowned his children and how many times in his teens he had told girlfriends to 'get rid of it.' How could he be sure he hadn't slept with any other of his offsprings?

Nico could see his idrin's ghostly face as he walked towards him, and knew that this was much more than the usual 'woman problem.' He braced himself for anything, yet he was nearly knocked off he his bar stool when Conteh told him just how serious it was.

"This is the pits, bredrin. Certainly not something you repeat with comfort," Nico reassured him. "De lid have to be tight on dis one, star."

"Just when I thought my troubles were coming to a fucking end, man! Shit.

Learning Centre
City and Islington Sixth Form College
283-309 Goswell Road
London EC1V 7LA

TWELVE

Conteh's reoccurring nightmares had started again, and it had begun to affect him bad. Another retreat to Jamaica crossed his mind, but it wasn't practical at the moment.

The incest thing had finally done it for him. Wiped him out, like a hurricane on an unsuspecting island. It was the writing on the wall. Like someone or some force was seriously trying to tell him something. Enough was enough, however late the realisation, it had well and truly come. He had made up his mind and hoped his decision hadn't come too late. He hoped his past would stay buried for good and wouldn't come back to haunt him. It was haunting enough just thinking about it.

Simone could not remember the last time that she had gone out to a nice restaurant to have a meal with her husband. It felt like the first time. It was her surprise treat. She drove him to the restaurant of her choice. She would have been disappointed had she known that her dear sweet husband had already christened the plush eats with Menna, a wickedly sexy woman he had fallen in love with.

"What will it be then beautiful people?" Loxley's friendly hospitality was on display again. He recognised Conteh from the last time he was in, but could not help noticing that his female partner was different. It came as no surprise though, since he saw this kind of thing all the time.

"We're still trying to decide." Simone smiled up at Loxley, then proceeded to examine the exquisite menu. "What about this Fish Escovitch Brean, stuffed with escallion and seasoning then?" Simone asked as she played with Conteh's fingers across the table.

"Sounds good," he replied.

"...And the Secret Garden Combi for starters." She looked at Conteh. "Come on. What d'you fancy? Secret Garden Combi: layer of ackee and callaloo wrapped in filo pastry case, covered with tomatoes and sweet pepper coulis? Fish Escovitch Brean, stuffed with escallion and seasoning? Chicken Kingston, fricassee style? Conteh? What's wrong with you?"

"Nothing, babes. Just a bit tired."

Simone believed him since he had played out the previous night. It was 5am before he was in bed and he had to be up at eight to pick Janet up from the airport. She was back from her six months vacation in Jamaica. It didn't cross Simone's mind that Conteh was suffering from an acute dose of guiltitis and a bad case of nerves.

Yes. An ill wind from his past had blown in to the restaurant. In the form of Menna, accompanied by Garnet, Conteh's ex next door neighbour! Garnet, whose left behind pie Conteh had so enjoyed tasting. He would never have put Garnet down as Menna's type. Not at all. Garnet was ugly. Too ugly. Even though he no longer had his dreadlocks. Even now that he had removed a forest of hair from his face. He dressed differently too. More conventional. The man was dapper. But anyway you looked at it, Garnet was out of Menna's reach. It was burning Conteh's raas. But he couldn't do a damn thing.

"Why don't we move to that corner seat over there, honey? Seems cosier." Conteh could hardly breathe.

"Why not. If it makes you happy." Simone rolled her eyes playfully.

"Decided yet?" Loxley was back and was pleased to know that they had. Conteh felt weird when he sat eating the very same meal he had with Menna on his last visit to the restaurant.

Conteh nearly choked on his Chicken Kingston. A sure-footed Menna was walking purposely, it seemed, towards his table.

"Are you all right, darling? Shall I get you some water?" Simone was concerned. Conteh had turned a lighter shade of dark. He looked like a dead man, ready for the bone yard. Especially when Menna paused behind Simone's chair and stared him straight in the eyes, with a serious attitude.

At first, she was surprised to see him too. It was his choking that drew her attention. She was on her way to the ladies, which was in the direction of his table.

"Yeah. I'm fine," Conteh said to Simone. "Went down the wrong hole, babes."

He averted his eyes from Menna's gaze as she walked back past his table. But even in his state of shock, he couldn't help but take another look at the ass that was once his. Even in that serious state of shock, the man rose... down below.

Conteh was still suffering from shock as Simone drove him home in her Beema. It was around midnight when she pulled into their road. Blue flashing lights met them as they drew closer. There was a fire engine outside their house. Firemen busied themselves extinguishing fire from the burning car on their drive. Conteh's Beema.

"Oh my god, Conteh! What happened?!"

Simone swung her Beema up onto the pavement a little distance away from the house and jumped out. Conteh jumped out too. Dazed.

"Stay back, miss," a policeman came towards Simone.

"What happened?!" she asked.

"Seems like arson. This container was on your lawn. It had petrol in it."

Simone stared at the empty container and then at the firemen as they busied themselves putting out the flames that engulfed her husband's pride and joy.

Conteh arrived at the scene like he was all drugged up. He couldn't say a word.

"Are you all right, sir?"

"Am I all right?! Am I all right?!" He sounded like a scratched record. "Am I fucking all right? That was my fucking car! My fucking car! Now it's a burnt out wreck!"

Conteh's shoulders slumped, he fell down on his knees and sobbed. Being soft had nothing to do with it. He heaved his Chicken Kingston from the pit of his stomach, onto the classy jacket Marcia had brought him back from Paris.

He could do without the neighbours too. He knew they meant well, but he could do without their commiserations. "I'm really sorry, Conteh... You must be gutted, mate," one neighbour was saying. "Oh well, at least the insurance will pay it... You are insured aren't you, mate?"

Pretty words couldn't help him. This hurt real bad. He choked with anger. His feelings could not be put into words.

"Who could have done this, babes?" he asked Simone later, after he had cleaned himself up. "Who could have done this? This is fuckries, man?"

Simone hugged and tried to comfort him. "Your guess is as good as mine, Conteh. Are you sure you haven't upset anyone lately?" she asked.

"Not that I know of." He had to lie. Conteh could have given her a list of people he had upset lately but, of course, he wouldn't.

Conteh freaked out the more he thought about it. Now he wished he had been a bit more careful with Marcia's little donation. That was history, every last penny. He had to find some story for Simone. How could he tell her he wasn't insured for that luxury on wheels? The white leather interior. The top of the range stereo system, with CD player. The 24-carat gold plated gear stick, engraved with his initials, CG. He was pig-sick. Conteh mopped his brows with the palm of his left hand, and filled his brandy glass with his right. He had all he could take for one night.

THIRTEEN

Conteh found himself in a room, tied to a bed with a wad of condoms stuffed into his mouth. Joya, Collette, Carmen were sat at the bottom of the bed loving it, and the smirks on their faces showed how much. Conteh was nude, his manhood protruded forth, unable to multiply. The door burst open, and in walked Menna and Marcia. Menna flashed a whip fiercely and loudly and Marcia held a shiny blade to his dick. The thought pained him.

"Hurry up, queen bee!" Menna was shouting to someone on the outside. "Let's get this bastard sorted."

Conteh shitted himself. Literally. Simone walked in, also with a whip. Conteh nearly choked on his mouthful of condoms. With her right arm hugging her waist and her left moulding her chin, Simone looked at Conteh, then at his dick, then she said, "Do it."

Conteh tried to scream but no sound came from his mouth. With one swipe, Marcia severed Conteh's dick, held it up with disdain between the tip of her long red fingernails, like she was examining a goat fish, and said, 'Souvenir anyone?'

They released him and as he ran from the room, dickless, Simone lashed her whip at his bare ass. He ran towards his car, leaving an echo of laughter behind. It was only when he got inside the car and slammed the door shut, that he realised it was on fire. He couldn't get out.

The central locking refused to open. He looked up at the window of the house from which he had just fled, and saw the faces of the women who had just tortured him. Their laughter penetrated his already tormented head. Where his dick was supposed to be, was covered with maggots of every shape and size.

"Are you okay, Conteh?" Her husband's screams had woken Simone. She shook him to consciousness. Conteh woke in a cold sweat and found himself punching hard at the wall of the bedroom. "Shit," he said when he realised it was only a dream.

"Not that same dream again?" asked Simone.

"Yeah. This is crazy," Conteh lied. This dream was different. In fact, he wouldn't tell her about the dream he had the previous night either, in which a cloaked figure dressed in black revealed the words AIDS written across his chest. It freaked Conteh out.

"I can't believe this dream is still haunting you. It's really weird," said Simone, sounding tired. "I seriously think you should consider seeing a psychiatrist about it. It's been haunting you for too long now."

Conteh ignored Simone's words and walked to the shower. He needed to wake himself up. It was 4am but he didn't want to sink into a sleep again. His subconscious was playing serious havoc with his head. *Feh real.*

Pam was deeply distressed when she called Simone, and Simone thought, 'This is all I need.' What could it be now? First some maniac had so much pent-up anger against her husband, they took it out on his car, and now her best mate had something so distressing to tell her, she couldn't tell her over the phone.

"I'll be there as soon as I can, darling," Simone assured her. She had just washed her hair and was in the middle of blowdrying it. She half-dried it in order to stop it tangling too much and decided to leave the *Dark and Lovely* treatment until later. As she climbed into her car, she couldn't help but notice the remaining blackness on the drive from the fire that took the shine off Conteh's night at The Xaymaca Experience.

Simone found Pam in a worst state than she expected.

"You are HIV positive?! Pam, are you sure?" Simone sat down on the edge of her best mate's settee and hugged her soft brown shoulders.

"Yes. I'm sure. Unless they gave me the wrong result." She paused. "That's wishful thinking. It's true, Simone." Pam looked into her best mate's eyes. "I'm going to die from what I loved the most. Sex. I suppose it's too late to listen to you now, eh Sim'?"

"What made you go for the test?" Simone searched for something to say.

"Remember Gary Parkes?"

"The First Officer?" Simone asked.

"Yes. He didn't die of pneumonia after all. It was AIDS. I spent a night in his hotel room on a stopover in Orlando some time ago. Skin to skin."

"But I thought he was engaged to..." Simone searched for the name.

"Yvonne Smith?" Pam helped her along. "Yes. Engaged and fucking bisexual. I didn't know this until after I slept with him. Thought it was strange, though, when he was more interested in my back passage than he was anywhere else. I kept guiding him, thinking he was simply missing, but after a while I realized that it was deliberate. He was only interested in anal sex. I should have insisted that that was a 'no go' zone."

The enormity of the situation began to dawn on Simone. If Gary had infected Pam, then Yvonne was at risk, in which case so was First Officer Bryant, since they had a fling last summer. First Officer Bryant's wife Nicole, was therefore also at risk. Little did Simone realize that this meant that she was at risk too. Because Pam had slept, unintentionally, with Conteh.

Pam was whimpering "Sorry Simone. I'm so sorry. I didn't know. I didn't know. Honestly."

"Of course you didn't know, darling. If a man is engaged to a woman, you automatically think that he's straight. How are you suppose to know that he's bisexual." How could Simone begin to imagine that her best friend was simply trying to say that she didn't know that the man she screwed after a dance some time back, was her husband? How could Pam tell her, when this was her nearest and dearest friend? The one who spent the most time telling her, 'If you can't be good, be careful."

"No. I couldn't know." Pam gathered herself. Thought better of it. Not through selfishness, but she would take the easy way out. After all, Conteh was no angel. Pam knew he had a string of women whom he had slept with in the past. She also knew that he was partial to riding bareback. Anyone of his concubines could have infected him with the AIDS virus. Statistics had shown that a high level of the population of Birmingham was already infected. Chances were, she might have already been too late where Conteh's downfall was concerned.

Simone wouldn't hear about the affair from her, she decided. She would inform Conteh and he would have to tell his wife. That was his duty..

"It won't necessarily develop into full-blown AIDS." Simone had almost every finger crossed for this one. Death was a thought she'd rather eliminate from her mind.

"Whatever happens, darling, you know you've got a friend." Simone's voice trembled as she struggled to fight back the tears.

"I know, babes."

The girls hugged again. Simone could no longer hold back the tears that had buckled behind her tear ducts.

"This place is a mess, Pam said suddenly, as if they'd just been talking about dinner. She gathered up the empty glasses on the coffee table and hurried to the kitchen. Simone admired her strength and didn't question it. "Are you still trying for that love child?" Pam shouted from the kitchen.

"No. No. We're not." Simone didn't want to talk about bringing a new life into the world, when it was possible that her best friend might be on her way out of it.

Pam was sinking slowly into thoughts of her Welsh mother and her Jamaican father, the coupled essences of her beauty, when Simone entered the kitchen.

"Are you okay, Pam?"

"Sure. Sure I am," she said, her eyes glazed with tears.

Menna gathered a pile of red silk sheets from her bedroom and piled them into a black bin bag. She looked around her flat for anything else that would remind her in the slightest of Conteh. It was their anniversary. The day she first walked into his shop, looking for a diamond ring.

She piled, too, into that black bin bag, desperate, irate, nasty, cussing letters from both Conteh and Nico. Poorly written letters expressing their anger at being given a taste of their own 'midicine'(sic).

The ritual burning of the sheets. A transition from the past, and Angie had agreed for her to do it in her garden.

Menna lay a single red rose upon the pile of silk. The lighter fluid and the flick of the match awakened something in Menna's head.

Angie looked on from beside her.

"Isn't it funny," Menna said, without averting her eyes from the raging flames, "how nothing is ever what it seems?" She smiled now. More of a sad grimace.

"Tell me about it," Angie agreed, waiting for Menna to explain what she meant.

"How nasty that silk would feel on my skin now," said Menna. She folded her arms across her chest and sighed. "It used to feel so nice. And that red. That rich red. Look how it changes now. The shade. Look how the fire changes it to a darker shade of red. Unlike the first time we lost ourselves between them."

Angie understood now. "Come on in, girl. Let's have a cup of tea."

"Haven't you got anything stronger than that?"

"Of course," replied Angie. Menna had buried the past. Angie hoped that the next door that opened for her friend, would be inviting, comforting, and habitable.

"Your mate has not flipped Ang'," Menna hugged her friend. "I had to do that, understand?"

"You don't have to explain, darling," Angie assured her, reaching for a glass of Tia Maria she had poured earlier.

The clink of their glasses sealed a moment. "To strong women. Women who are willing to move on." Menna toasted.

Angie smiled meaningfully and said, "I'm gonna miss you, girl."

"It's only six months. I'll write. Even call occasionally. You won't get rid of me that easy." Menna reached for a familiar CD as she spoke.

Weren't you the one who tried to hurt me with goodbyes?
Did I crumble? Did I lay down and die?

Gloria Gaynor did it again for her.

Holding the now half-filled glass in her hand, Menna danced around Angie's living room. Every shimmy of her hips, every twist of her waist, every snap of her fingers, every smile, every breath said:

The last laugh will be the haughtiest.

Angie watched and was happy for her.

FOURTEEN

There was a robbery at All That Glitters, the jewellers right opposite Conteh's shop. The owner, Joe Callaghan, was forced at gunpoint to load his gems into a black sack. The hooded and masked robber did not speak, simply gesturing with his gun. A slight gape in his gloves revealed that he was of African-Caribbean descendant.

The rest of the radio news didn't interest Conteh. There were already too many things on his mind to take on another tribulation, and the last thing he wanted was a robbery, or a break-in. He floored the gas pedal of his hire car, and burned towards his shop.

Conteh sighed with relief when he arrived and found that his shop and its contents were in tact. Across the road, police were swarming all over All That Glitters, with fingerprint experts dusting the place down.

"Hey, Joe. Sorry to hear about your shit, man. I only just heard the news." Conteh called out.

Joe Callaghan looked up and started crossing the road towards Conteh. The always-jolly Irish man had lost his spark. Under the circumstances, it was to be expected.

Conteh shook Jim's hand and felt his anger.

"What can you do," he replied. "Fucking black bast...!" Jim stopped in his tracks as he realised that Conteh was also made in the shade. "Look, mate, oi'm sorry. The colour of the robber has not'ing to do wid it. He could have been any colour. It's just dat oi'm angry, Conteh."

Conteh could tell just how angry Jim was. His accent had become stronger.

"Who wouldn't be, Jim? Who wouldn't be? I'm just glad you didn't get hurt, man."

"I can't even tell you to be careful, Conteh. How can anyone be careful wit' a gun pointed at your head? Be-Jeezus." Jim's face became redder, flushed with anger.

"For real, Jim. For real. Listen, mate, I've got to go. I just hope they catch the... bastard."

"A tell you," added Jim, "if oi get me hands on 'im, oi'll be doing toime for murder."

"Jim. Take it easy, man." Conteh shook his hand again and the men went about their businesses.

The woman that walked into Conteh's shop just before closing time, was as weird as any black female he had ever seen. She wore a long blonde wig that covered most of her face, and a ton of make-up that would need a shovel to remove. Her green eyes reminded him of next door's cat and he was convinced she was battery operated.

"Looking for anything special?" Conteh forced himself to be polite.

"Just browsing, thanks." Even her accent seemed artificial.

He kept his eye on her discreetly, as he answered the shop phone. It was Simone, and he welcomed the sound of her voice.

"Conteh Gonzalez?"
The police were waiting for him when he arrived to open

up The Golden Touch the following morning. One white cop, and a black cop who gave Conteh a 'We're not brothers now, mate,' look. They flashed their warrant cards.

"Yes. Can I help you officers?"

"We have a warrant to search your premises in connection with the robbery at All That Glitters a few days ago."

"You what?!" This is a joke, right?" Conteh was flabbergasted.

Conteh checked the date on his watch. It wasn't April 1. This wasn't a joke.

"Don't suppose you know anything about the content of this bag, do you, sir?" The black officer pulled a heavy bag from under a display unit.

"How did that get there? No. I've never seen it before in my life." He thought back quick. "There was this woman here just before I locked up last night. I took my eye off her for only a second... It must have been her."

The officers looked at each other, clearly doubting his story.

The black officer revealed the content of the bag, and the white one read him his rights. Apparently, he didn't have that many:

"You have the right to remain silent but anything you say..."

"I said, some woman left it here! Which part of that didn't you guys understand?"

Conteh was flogging a dead horse. The boys in blue weren't interested. All they were interested in was that the bag contained jewellery from All That Glitters, and a metal shooter, the same one that was held to Joe Callaghan's head the day before.

"It's not happening. This shit is not fucking happening."

Conteh called his wife. Luckily, it was her rest day. He told her it looked bad, that if he didn't find that black mannequin he would surely be in hot callaloo. Like an unfortunate mosquito. *Feh real.*

"Said some woman left the nicked goods in his shop, sarge."

"Did he now. I suppose she did the robbery too, and after going to all that trouble, walked across the road and said, 'Here you are, look after this for me, will you. It's got bells on it. I hope, Mr Gonzalez, you have a damn good lawyer."

From his cell, Conteh heard the laughter of the officers. He prayed that there really was a God, and that his mother's good service history would put him in good stead for the help he would need. He hoped that God would help the boys from Bramblewood and Milligrip Solicitors to prove his innocence.

"What have I done to deserve this, Conteh?" Simone's eyes filled with tears. "First your car, then my best friend tells me she's HIV positive, then you get arrested for some absurd crime. What the hell am I gonna hear next?"

"Pam is HIV positive? Fuck..." Conteh looked like death warmed up. Simone's visit had brought more bad news than he could bear. For the past few months, his world seemed to have been crumbling around him. Now here he was behind bars for something he didn't do, hearing that some woman he screwed on the sly, was HIV positive!

"Yes, she is. I know it's hard to believe, but you don't know her like I do. She can be reckless and carefree at times. She lives on the edge. If only she'd listened to me. I didn't want her to stop having fun, but to protect herself while she was doing it. It doesn't just end there. She has slept with other people as well who could be infected." Simone paused. She felt guilty for rattling on about Pam, when her husband had grave problems of his own.

Conteh was thinking, too. A song flashed in his head like an electric shock:

If you are a big, big tree
there is a small axe
sharpen ready
ready to cut you down
ready to cut you down.

He was the big tree, Conteh knew, and AIDS the small axe.

"Is she sure she's HIV?" Conteh needed to double check.

"Of course she is. She took the test. HIV and AIDS aren't things you tell anyone about unless you're really sure. Remember me telling you that one of our colleagues died of pneumonia a while ago?"

"Yeah. Yeah." Conteh was anxious.

"Well, it wasn't pneumonia. It was AIDS. Pam slept with him. Anyway, let's talk about the reason you're in this god-forsaken place."

Simone didn't realise that being in jail for robbery had suddenly become the least of Conteh's problems. All that he could think of was the day he screwed Pam, and how she climaxed all over his dick, with pleasure.

"Simone, I swear I didn't sleep with... I mean, I swear I had nothing to do with this robbery. That bitch left those things in my shop. It's a set-up. Believe me."

For once, Simone believed him. She knew he was a lying, cheating, womanising bastard, but she felt sure that he didn't have it in him to pull off such a thing, and then to be so stupid as keep the evidence in his own shop. Although she believed him, she was neither judge nor jury and, right then, that was all that mattered — what they believed. She couldn't even provide an alibi since she was on a flight at the time of the robbery.

Conteh's brain was in a spin. He had to tell his dear wife that he had slept with her best friend, unprotected, and could have infected her as well? But how? Would there be a good time to tell her? If he told her, Simone wouldn't be his loving wife anymore. Now when he needed her to do everything in her power to get him out of this dump. Maybe he should simply let sleeping dogs lie.

It didn't stop there. It got worse the more he thought about it. Carmen, Joya, Collette, Beverley, Mitzi and his own daughter Cerise who he slept with without the knowledge that he was her father, could all be infected. If he told Simone, he would have to tell them all. How could he face them? And then there was the child he fathered and grandfathered at the same time. And all the other women he had slept with after Pam.

Then there was Nico... The web got thicker by the minute and he could not bear it any longer.

"I'll see you in two weeks, Conteh." Simone got up from the chair and brushed the back of her skirt.

"Come back soon, babes." Conteh couldn't bear to look at the back of his wife disappearing, leaving him on his own to face the cell that was to be his home for a while yet.

Conteh sat down on his uncomfortable rubber mattress and prayed for three things. That Simone would wait, that he wouldn't have the AIDS virus and that he would be proven innocent.

Now he needed his God. Real bad.

She was well away. Nobody knew that she had robbed the jewellery store. Nobody knew that she had set Conteh up. Conteh would, eventually, when he had stewed in jail long enough. He would realise that he had been played. Menna's ears pricked up. It was the final call to her flight. She picked up her vanity case and headed for gate number 13. "Lucky for some," she muttered to herself. As she boarded the Air Jamaica jet, she felt light. As if a weight had been lifted from her shoulders. She needed a break and could think of no better place to take it than the place of her birth. She had given up her job as editor with *Black Star Magazine* and opted for six months in the sun. She could afford it. Besides, where better could she finish her first novel, than under the shade of a palm tree, sipping Malibu, drawing inspiration from golden horizons and dancing waves?

"Business or pleasure?" Sex Appeal himself spoke to her.

She couldn't help but notice his Rolex watch. She had already noticed his Calvin Klein attire and wafted his alluring fragrance, also Calvin Klein's — 'a compelling invitation to bed', she smiled.

Before she answered his question, she checked out his shoes too. It was a strange ritual she had developed. It was her friend Angie who once told her, 'When you meet a man, check out his shoes.' Menna wouldn't swear by it, but in a funny kind of way, it became a compulsive action — like not walking under a ladder, or being careful not to spill salt.

The man was clearly a fashion victim, but who was complaining?

"Excuse me?" Menna delivered one of her 'You'll have to work hard with this one' look.

"Your trip to JA? Is it business or pleasure?" He knitted his brows, showing a slight perplexity. "I'm sure I've seen you somewhere before." He paused. "Yeah. That's it… In _Black Star Magazine_? You're the editor. Not article hunting are we?"

"No." Menna smiled. "Both. Business and pleasure."

"Waiting for you out there is he?" You would think he would have stretched the conversation a bit longer before checking for dead-end streets.

"_He?_" Menna had been down this road so many times before.

"The man," he replied. "I can't believe any sensible man would allow a sexy thing like you to go away by herself.

Especially to JA. The guys out there are suckers for sexy ladies like you, y'know."

Menna smirked. There she was in a pair of jeans and baggy T-shirt, and she was sexy. Well, she didn't feel it. She figured it must be 'in the eyes of the beholder'.

"Do you always assume there has to be a man in the life of every female you see travelling alone?" Menna's tone was laced with attitude. Facetiness.

"No. But I sure can't be wrong in my assumption." The hunk wasn't backward in coming forward. Not in the least.

"How about you?" Menna asked, turning the table. "Does _she_ feel safe letting you travel alone?"

"There isn't a 'she'." He sipped his drink suggestively.

Menna started fantasising about love at first flight.

"And I don't believe that pigs fly either." Menna continued being facety.

"I'm serious. Why would I lie?" Now he looked her straight in the eyes.

"Because you're a man."

"Woo! Woo!" He emitted the sexiest chuckle. "Sounds like a lady who's met a trickster or two in the past. Listen, sista, don't tar every black man with that same infamous dog brush. There are some good ones out there, you know. We're not all like these bastard men you women talk about?" He readied himself for deep conversation.

"Did _I_ mention bastard men?" Menna pointed to herself.

"You don't have to. It's laced all over your tone."

His body language stirred something inside her and made her want to pull right back into her safe zone. He was too smooth, too slick, too sexy. This seemed like trouble again. Besides, it was too soon. If she didn't put the brakes on, she would find herself falling for this guy in a big way. Talk about rebound!

Sex Appeal's name was Clinton. They chatted non-stop about Jamaica, Menna's work, his work, countries they'd visited, hoped to visit, people they'd met and people they would like to meet. They had been airborne for an hour or so when a steward, too pretty to be a man, interrupted their conversation with his overflowing trolley. "Drink, madam? Sir?"

"A Tia Maria for me." Menna didn't hesitate.

"I'll have a Bacardi and Coke." Clinton looked at Menna with the look of a chicken coming home to roost. He felt quite certain he had pulled. He was already fantasising about their romps between the sheets. Fantasising was how they both drifted off to sleep, somewhere high above the Atlantic.

Menna woke and found Clinton snoring slightly, a square white card had fallen out of the book he was reading. She picked it up with the intention of replacing it, but curiosity got the better of her and she couldn't help but read the purposeful words:

Just thought I'd slip this in to remind you who you left behind.

Don't be careful, just be GOOD. See you in a fortnight.

Love Chantelle. XXX.

The discovery didn't surprise her. Looking over at the snoring beast who was earlier a gorgeous hunk, she turned the family snap over and beheld an image of togetherness.

Clinton was embracing a beautiful woman. The face looked familiar. Menna looked even closer. 'Fuck,' she thought, 'Chantelle Morgan!' She could hardly believe her eyes. Chantelle had stood behind her five years previously in a graduation line-up, as they both picked up their BA Honours degrees in Media and Communications Studies. She could almost hear Chantelle's lilting voice singing Clinton's praises back then. The man she thought was faithful to the max, and only had eyes for her.

Clinton stirred. Menna quickly slipped the photo back into his book and replaced it. She stared at his face, she could almost hear him barking. Dog. 'A narrow escape,' she mumbled to herself. 'A narrow, fucking escape.'

When Clinton woke, he was hoping to pick up from where they left off.

"I can't believe we're nearly there," he smiled smoothly. "Amazing. This must be the quickest nine hours I've ever spent. Must be the company.

Menna gave him her 'attitude' look.

He noticed.

"So. Am I going to see you again?"

"Why not?" Menna perked up. Like a soldier on a battlefield. Ammunition poised. "We seem to have a lot in common. Conversation-wise at least. I think the friendship is worth a bash. Besides, ambitious men like yourself are hard to find these days."

"True. True." Clinton was pleased, and as if it was a fresh thought, he reached into his inside pocket and produced a business card. *Executive Producer. Ebony Greeting Cards.* It had his office and mobile number. "Don't lose it. Call me." He spoke with authority

"Oh, I will," Menna promised. "You can count on it."

That cheered him up immensely.

"I still can't believe there isn't a man in your life." Clinton's curiosity surfaced again.

"That feeling is mutual, Clinton. I can't believe there isn't a woman in your life."

"Straight up. I'm a single guy, I'm alone and I'm a single guy, just need a sweet loving woman to lean on."

'Fuck. The man sings as good as he lies,' Menna was thinking.

"I like your style, Clinton."

He held her hand, presumed he could kiss her cheek.

"You can be sure that there's no man in my life," she continued. "But there is a woman. I'm gay. You've got no hang-ups on having a gay friend have you?"

She could feel the cold as he froze. He fidgeted. His eyes shifted, his palms sweated and his body spoke another language. He wanted to wipe the lips that had just kissed her.

"You're... _gay?_"

"Yeah. Homophobic are you, Clinton?"

"No. No. It's just that..."

"It's just that you've never met a gay black woman before? You see, Clinton, brothas have been shits for too long, sistas are turning this love thing in on themselves. Better dividends."

Clinton mopped his brow. He had to be dreaming.

"Still. You seem different. Genuine. You might even be able to re-bend my gender," Menna continued. "I'll call you." She smirked now at the back of Clinton's head. He was now looking to his right, at the Frank Bruno lookalike, who couldn't help over-hearing the conversation. The sturdy man was trying not to smile, but with great difficulty.

"I... I don't know if it's such a good idea after all," Clinton turned to Menna, like a shamed dog. She had flopped him good and proper. The rahtid liar.

"Why? No longer fancy the idea of getting into my knickers, Clinton? Or is it because another woman has been eating from a plate you had designs on?" Menna didn't moderate her voice.

Clinton was now lost for words. He wanted the floor of the jet to open up and let him fall out. He leant back in his seat and hoped Menna would do the right thing and return his business card. In fact, he hoped she wouldn't say another word to him.

She didn't. At least not then.

It wasn't long before the jet touched down in Jamaica. Menna's brother was waiting for her at the airport. Clinton caught her eyes as she entered the waiting Lexus. He turned away quickly, in disgust, but had to look her way again just as quick, when she shouted, "Clinton, give my love to Chantelle. And don't forget, don't be careful, just be GOOD. Ciao!" With that she blew him a seductive kiss.

"What was dat all about, sis?" her brother had recognised the sting in her voice.

"Nothing," she replied, smirking like a hooker who had just stripped a punter's wallet dry. "Nothing."

As she peered at the floating clouds, the sun-lit sky and

the picturesque scenes that floated by as they drove away from the airport, Menna wondered who wrote the words; 'Nature kissed the earth and called it Jamaica.' Then she closed her eyes for a moment and daydreamed only of the island's good side. Its sandy beaches, palm trees, waterfalls and blue oceans — its paradise. Then the sweet hunger for her grandmother's ackee and saltfish, surrounded by a bed of succulent roast breadfruit, to be washed down with tasty hot chocolate, haunted her taste buds.

Her brother noticed the lingering gloating expression on Menna's face. "What yuh up to, sis? Who was dat guy? Yuh been smiling like a' don't know what ever since we lef' the airport."

Clinton was the least of Menna's thoughts. She closed her eyes, licked her lips and almost tasted the sweet taste of revenge. Earlier, back in England, she thanked Sharon, her blonde assistant. For the leggy blonde, too, justice was done. This was no dumb blonde, for she was clever enough to whip the hot tape out of Nico's camera as the two dogs slept. Menna had more than she had bargained for. As for the robbery she pulled off single-handedly, she would be licking her own ass for a while.

Menna sucked her teeth. It was no point explaining anything to her brother. She loved him, but he was a man. A man who had broken more than his fair share of hearts. Being her brother didn't set him apart from the rest.

"How's my dear gran'madda?" she asked.

"Strong like an ox," her brother replied.

"How's her proverbial tongue, bro'? Still sharp?"

"Sharper than ever, sis."

"Just get me to her will you. Fast."

A pleasure-filled smirk invaded Menna's face, and her own mutterings cascaded gently, a wonder to her ears: 'Revenge is sweet. Sweeter than a black man's dick.' She had got some sweet revenge on Conteh and, true, it was much sweeter than his penis.

Simone noticed the flash car pulling up in front of her house. BMW Z3 Sport. Red. She thought she wouldn't mind owning one herself. A beautiful black woman climbed out of the vehicle and proceeded to walk up the drive. Simone went to her front door in anticipation. She opened.

"Yes? Can I help you?" She was now looking at the woman in full. This female had class. Real class. And she either had a sugar daddy, or a fat bank account.

The stranger on the doorstep looked Simone up and down like a slave master examining a slave he was about to buy. "Hi," she said simply. "You are beautiful." Her left arm enfolded her thin waistline. The thumb and index finger of her right hand gently manipulated her chiselled chin.

Simone wondered if this woman had looked at herself lately. 'How could a woman like this call *me* beautiful', she thought.

"Who are you?" Simone was curious.

"Where is *he*?" The woman evaded her question.

"Where's who?"

"Conteh. Lover boy." Her voice was hatefully sweet.

"Excuse me?"

"You mean he didn't tell you about me? My name is Marcia. You're Simone. I know. I've been fucking your husband."

Simone was stunned, didn't know what to do, but knew that she didn't want her dirty laundry hung out on th e doorstep for all to see.

"C-c-come in Marcia... Come in. Would you like a drink?"

"Brandy. Straight. Thank you," Marcia said, following Simone into the house and through to the living room.

"Sit down, Marcia." Simone tried to hide her uneasiness.

"No thank you. I'm not stopping."

Marcia knocked back the brandy neat. The expression on her face changed, like a cluster of broken clouds passing under a stormy sky. "I fell in love you know." She spoke now with a frozen grin. "I didn't mean to, but I did. All I needed was someone to give me orgasms at first. That was all I needed. Just for him to make me come. Honest." Now the seemingly confident woman rocked her head from side to side and cried like a baby.

"Marcia, are you okay?"

"Yes, I'm okay. I've come here to get my fucking twenty grand back."

"Twenty grand?" Simone was puzzled.

"I can see why he wouldn't leave you." Marcia's eyes became glazed. "No wonder. You're fucking amazing." Marcia fixed her gaze on Simone and approached her slowly. "He wouldn't leave you for me. You didn't know that did you? Said he loved you. Said he would never leave you. You bitch!"

Now Simone found herself up against the wall, her head hard against a ticking cuckoo clock. Marcia's hands grabbed her breasts, gripping them tight.

"Liked these did he?" She spoke in an evil whisper. "Screwed him good did you? And I bet you have red silk sheets, too."

A surge of bile filled Simone's trembling mouth as Marcia grabbed her private. She could not believe what she had let into her house. Was she completely mad? Did she want to rape her?

"What are you doing? Get off me!" Simone found some strength to protest, but was confused when Marcia switched again. She released her and said softly, "I have to go, Simone. I have to go now."

Marcia headed for the door and to her car.

"I'll be back," she promised.

Simone was glad when Janet picked up the phone. Apart from Pam, if there was anyone she could talk to in situations like this, it was her sister-in-law.

"Simone. What's up?" Janet was pleased to get a call from her sister-in-law. It had been a terrible time for them all since Conteh got banged up, and everyone was trying their best to cope.

Simone poured out her grief.

"What!" Janet was trying to take in what Simone was telling her about her encounter with Marcia. 'Marcia', she remembered that name.

"The thing is, Janet," Simone continued, "she was definitely not all there. It's so strange. The way she touched me. Then she said something about wanting her money back."

Janet wasn't completely surprised. She remembered the threat to Conteh on her note in Jamaica:*You're gonna pay.*

But she didn't expect anything like the incident Simone had described.

"Did you call the police?"

"No. No... I didn't. I think it's a case for the mental hospital, Jan. I really do. The woman is sick. She needs help."

"...That brother of mine."

"That reminds me," Simone added, "I forgot to ask you..."

Janet knew what was coming. At least she was on the end of a telephone line. She wouldn't have liked to lie in Simone's face.

"Conteh said you lost a gold and black earring the last time you were down? Is that right?"

"Yeah. Yeah, Simone. I did." Janet felt ashamed to have to lie to her sister-in-law, especially as she felt that it was in vain. Simone was hardly going to forgive Conteh after Marcia's revelations.

"...Are you still there? Simone?"

"Yeah. I'm here. Listen, Janet, I've got to go now. It's been a long day. I'll speak to you soon. Thanks for listening."

Janet ended the conversation apprehensively. She could feel a strange difference in Simone's tone.

Simone replaced the receiver and walked over to a drawer that held a single red earring. She flipped the lid of her bin and dropped it in with disdain. After all, it couldn't be Janet's. The rightful owner wasn't an issue now. It didn't matter anymore. This revelation was simply the final straw to a decision she should have made a long time ago. She removed the band of gold from her wedding finger.

FIFTEEN

Simone must have picked up the receiver no less than six times. She was contemplating calling the number on the card she had been holding for the past hour. It was several months since Lawrence had given her his card and he must have long gone told himself that she wouldn't call.

"Simone! Hi!" Lawrence's voice was a welcome sound.

She had finally picked up the courage to call.

The following night she met him for dinner.

"What made you call?" Lawrence spoke to Simone across a cosy table for two in a plush restaurant in Solihull. They had already ordered and were waiting for their meal over glasses of expensive wine.

"I stumbled upon your card," Simone joked.

"Yeah. Right." Lawrence displayed a set of perfect white teeth and his cute dimples made Simone want to caress him. YSL wafted around his space, encouraging her desire to handle him. "Now the real reason," he said. His voice was teasing, like foreplay.

"Is it a must that you know now, Lawrence? Can't we just enjoy our time together?" Her slender fingers rubbed the edge of her glass and the action teased him.

"Okay. Just as long as you tell me, eventually."

"Can I ask you a question? You don't have to answer if you don't want to." Simone looked into his eyes for permission.

"Feel free." He sipped his wine.

"Why did you say that I was emotionally strong?"

"Look, Simone, I'm no fool. When I first ask you out, you turned me down. From then, I respected you with a difference. Another woman, man or not, would have been game for a fling. Don't get me wrong. If you had accepted, I probably would have taken it. After all, I am a man. And you are beautiful. But I would have had reservations about taking you seriously."

"You haven't answered my question."

"From what I have gathered, you need to be emotionally strong to take what you've been getting." She stared transfixed at him. "But don't tell me," he continued, " you love him, right?"

Simone felt exposed. "So, who's been gossiping?"

"Is it a must that you know now, Simone? Can't we just enjoy our time together?" he teased. "I promise, I'm not trying to cut in on your husband or anything. Or Captain Ryce for that matter, 'cause he's got the hots for you, too, you know."

Simone raised an eyebrow.

"But I know one thing," Lawrence continued, "This is a once in a lifetime chance to take what I feel is the last jigsaw piece to make my life complete. It feels too right to let go. Of course, your husband wouldn't see it that way. He would simply see me as a sneaky, small island bastard who's trying to trip him up."

Simone chuckled.

The waiter approached their table with a tantalising dish of succulent chicken breast in white wine sauce.

"But if the feeling isn't mutual, I won't push it." Lawrence ignored the waiter's presence and carried on. "Please. Don't take my honesty for bullshitting. I know a gift horse when I see one. And a good woman is what I'm looking for." A slight residue of an Antiguan accent decorated his sexy tone.

"Isn't there anyone in your life, Lawrence?" She looked at this handsome, confident face and couldn't imagine him not loving, or not being loved, like a bottle of the best fragrance — wrapped and unused.

"Anyone? Or *anyone?*" he asked. "Put it this way, Simone, not anyone I'd like to marry. I'm forty-three years old and I am ready to settle down with a woman that moves something inside me. Yes, there is someone I'm sleeping with. But it's purely that. Everyone needs their bed warming from time to time. She knows exactly where it's at too." He was down with the best policy. Honesty.

They still hadn't touched their food. The conversation was more interesting.

"...That relationship can be severed anytime." Lawrence saw the look on Simone's face and felt he had to reassure her.

"Have you ever been married?" she asked.

"Yes. She was an American. I won't lie and tell you I didn't love her. I did. Big time. She left me for a rich Nigerian. Come on, let's eat. This food will be stone cold."

Simone picked up her cutlery and tried to picture this Nigerian. He must have been reeking much more than money, for the man that sat in front of her was drop-dead gorgeous. And, from where she was sitting, he was generating much more than good looks.

She wanted to hear more. The whens, the wheres, the whys and and wherefore. But now she would eat, drink and enjoy Lawrence's company.

The drive back from the restaurant was more than pleasant. Simone hadn't let Lawrence in too much on her thoughts but he knew that she wouldn't be sitting in his Mercedes if she didn't want to. He knew she was a virtuous woman, so when she allowed him to kiss her long and hard, and passionate, and outside her front door, too, he knew the way was beginning to clear for him.

Simone didn't invite him in for coffee. Until the divorce papers were signed sealed and delivered, she wouldn't bring another man under the roof that she and Conteh once shared. Unlike Conteh.

Simone stood on her doorstep and watched Lawrence drive off. The change she had deserved had finally come.

She closed the front door behind her and faced the remains of her life with Conteh. She fixed her eyes upon the wedding photo that graced the mantlepiece, next to the blown-up picture of herself and Conteh on a beach in Jamaica.

'Nothing lasts forever,' she thought.

It was 1am. The house was quiet, except for the ticking of the avant garde cuckoo clock they brought back from their trip to Switzerland last year. She sat down on the settee and rubbed her palm against its soft leather upholstery, remembering how they both decided on it together. Books about Martin Luther King, Malcolm X and Bob Marley on the bookshelf, opened up a new trail of thoughts — Conteh was an expert on the lives of the three legends, which contributed to many hours of conversation in the past. As she rubbed her palm against the settee, she wanted to ask, 'Why? Why? Why?'

Tears gathered in her eyes. The cuckoo clock ticked, and brought back the memory of Marcia. Again, Simone watched the video that the postman brought only this morning. The one that captured her lawful-wedded husband in compromising positions with a blonde and a brunette, and Nico, his partner in lust. Nico who sat at her table, ate with them and grinned in her face for the longest time. Earlier, she had viewed the video of Nico and her husband getting busy with a blonde.

Nico must have paced the whole length of the clinic's busy corridor. The short wait for the doctor seemed like hours, and his anxiety made him angry with everyone who happened to walk by wearing a white coat. It wasn't very often that the handsome (full of himself) hunk loses control, and he needed seriously to pull himself together.

An assertive asian doctor emerged from a door displaying the sign Dr. Singh and said, "Nicholas Kaur."

Nico's heart beat like an African drum and his palms became clammy with perspiration. As he walked through the waiting room towards the doctor, he glanced around to make sure there was no one sitting there that he knew.

"Take a seat, Mr Kaur," said the doctor.

Nico fidgeted nervously in his chair. His lips became dry and he began to wish he wasn't there at all. He had no doubt about the possibility of him being HIV positive. Pam was dying of AIDS and he had unprotected sex with her. Now he had two choices. Take each day as it comes and hope for the best, or be told and deal with it like the man he thought he was. The fact that he had found his way into the clinic, and was now sitting in front of a doctor, proved that he must have wanted to know the fact.

It wasn't long before a tube of blood was pulled from a willing vein. A tube of blood that held the verdict of his life. He was to return that afternoon for the result.

Nico knew it. A new doctor had replaced Dr Singh and he was over-nice.

"Cut the niceties, doc. Am I or aren't I?"

"I'm afraid your results are positive, Mr Kaur."

Nico heard nothing else after that. The voices and sounds around him became distant murmurs. His world had caved in. After what seemed like many hours later, he was floating down the long corridor and into the light of day, appreciating for the first time every breath and step he took, every sight he saw, every smell, every tree, every leaf and every cloud. There was no sense in being sorry now. The clock could not be reversed. The future was formidable. Threatening. Hanging there like a waiting gallows.

"Can you believe it, star?" Nico spoke to Conteh. "Can you believe this shit? Fucking HIV positive."

Conteh could believe it. He had managed to get a phone card and was ringing his spar from the nick. He had wanted Nico to go round and sound Simone out, find out how she was getting on with her campaign to prove his innocence. He had tried to call her several times, but he kept getting her answering machine. Phone cards were like gold dust inside.

Conteh would rather not have listened to Nico yakking on about this HIV shit. He had already been through what Nico was now going through, and had had time to think about it too. At least Nico wouldn't be spending the next ten years of his life banged up for a crime he didn't commit...

Nico managed a visit, but his heart was heavy. Conteh looked up from staring at his fingers to see new anger erupting on his spar's face.

"Easy rude bwoy. It's life. What can we do now? The only thing we can hope is that the youths that are coming up know the reality of this AIDS shit. When we were youths, we didn't have not'n to worry about. At least not'n that a dose of penicillin couldn't cure. Now it's different, star. Pleasure can fucking kill you. Look at us. The dons. Cut down in our fucking prime. Still. We've got ourselves to blame. Couldn't stand wearing condoms could we? Took the real feeling away didn't they? Now what's better? Half a feeling or none at all? There will be no skin to skin in the boneyard, star."

Conteh sounded like he was preaching. His words inflamed Nico's anger more. Conteh knew his idrin well and could almost read his thoughts, and they certainly weren't good ones.

"Don't do anything silly now, Nico. I know what you're thinking, bredrin. Feh real. Don't do it, man."

The warden had given the sign and Nico was now standing up. "Don't worry, bredrin. I'll see you in two weeks." There was a lump in his throat and he thumped a nearby wall as he walked away. "As the devil's my witness," he mumbled in anger, "I'm taking a few with me, or my name isn't Nicholas Kaur."

'Who Let the Dogs Out' was playing when Nico entered the club. Fern Gully. It was his new playground now. The Scratcher's Yard was still going, but it had lost that healthy vibe it generated when Conteh was around. But that wasn't the reason why Nico didn't go there anymore. Bad news had travelled fast, and tongues were wagging about him being HIV positive. He had denied it to all who dared to ask and since it wasn't written in his face, they simply had to draw their own conclusions.

The girl's at the Scratcher's Yard knew him well and all those who wanted a piece of his action before would now decline with pleasure. But he wasn't so known at Fern Gully, and the women there were suckers for handsome strangers. They would be drawn to him like mosquitoes to fresh blood.

Now he prowled through the unsuspecting crowd like The Predator.

"Can I have this dance?" Nico stretched his hand towards a Janet Jackson lookalike. He was in full swing. The Special Brews he had sunk earlier gave him the confidence he needed for a callous killing spree. This was his sixth prey, and he succeeded every time in getting that fatal dance. He had started on the ground floor, where ragga and jungle music lived, and now he was cooling out upstairs, where revives, lovers rock and calypso were the only things.

Nico had already accumulated five telephone numbers and it was a sure thing that he would obtain another few, before the night was out. The club was packed and the lights were low, black man style. The women whose numbers he had already taken would have a job picking up on his game. He had left them downstairs in different corners of the room, patiently waiting for him to return, but Nico had a mission to accomplish. He had granted himself his own licence to kill, and would not ease up.

Now he danced with the innocent chick, like slow poison. And that was exactly what he was. Slow poison. His dance was foreplay itself. He was a deadly mover and his preys would all want to taste the main course.

"It isn't fair, Nico. Isn't there enough damage done?"

It was Beverley, at his side like a thorn. She too was HIV positive, thanks to Conteh.

"What are you talking about, Beverley?" Nico held on to his dancing partner and leaned towards the fly in his soup.

"You know exactly what I'm taking about, Nico. The A. I. D. S virus?" Beverley spelt the letters out slowly..

The girl he was dancing with must have mistaken Beverley for an irate ex-girlfriend, and freed herself from Nico's grip.

"AIDS virus?" Nico played the innocent. "Don't know what yuh talking about."

"Look, Nico, don't come the innocent with me."

Beverley dragged on her cigarette. "I've watched you tonight and I can see exactly what you're doing. Take it like a man, Nico. It's your shit. These women did nothing to you."

Nico tried to smile a genuine smile, but Beverley could see the hardness behind his dry 'kin teet'.

"Listen," Beverley continued, "you're not my brother. I'm not even a close friend. I just screwed your best mate a few times. What you do with your life is nothing to do with me. All I'm saying is, it's fuckries what you're doing. Taking this thing out on a host of innocent women is not fair."

"I said, I don't know what you're talking about. I need a drink." Nico forced his way through the thick crowd in an attempt to get to the bar. Beverley kept her eyes on the back of his head, and when he got there, he turned and their eyes met. He had turned to see if she was still standing there. They stared at each other through the dimness of the room. Beverley wondered how many of the other ravers were HIV, how many had made a conscious decision to wipe out. The thought was too frightening to entertain. She shook her head then squeezed through tight openings, rubbing unintentionally against a sea of breasts, dicks and backsides to get to the narrow corridor that lead to the ladies' loo.

"Listen, darling," Beverley spoke to the woman that was dancing with Nico earlier. The unsuspecting beauty was powdering her nose, as if the difference could be seen in the dim room. "The guy you were just dancing with…" Without turning, the woman glared at Beverley's image through the mirror into which she was staring. "Just leave well alone will you?" she continued. "It's nothing to do with a jealous girlfriend, ex-girlfriend or anything. Just don't go there, girl. Don't give him your number. Don't take his. Take it from a sista. Me know what me talkin' about."

"Got a woman has he? Might have known. Men. They're all dogs." The woman pressed her lips together and returned her lipstick to her purse. "So, why yuh tellin' me dis?" She turned now to face Beverley.

"It's a long story, darling. Just count yourself lucky." Beverley felt like a Good Samaritan. Now she wished she had the balls to walk back into the room, demand the mike from the DJ and send out a warning. 'Why should it be so hard to do?' she had wondered. After all, she would do so if she knew of the inevitable fate of an exploding bomb.

"Men are shits aren't they?" As the woman left the small confinement of the ladies' loo, Beverley looked at her ass through her painted-on dress and knew she couldn't imagine how narrow her escape was. Now she studied her own reflection in the mirror and realised how much she had taken life for granted.

The DJ played 'Every woman deserves a good buddy.' "Like a fucking hole in the head," she muttered to herself, picking up on the blatant innuendo of the jolly calypso jive. She wiggled her ass to the cheeky number and was grateful she could do that. She didn't know how long it would last. For now, she would dance. "What the heck," she said, as she decided against replacing her lipstick. "What the fucking heck."

That night, Nico scored three times. He had found that the idea of one night stands was no longer a taboo to a host of women. This scenario helped his mission, with ease. The other four women he would get around to eventually. And the search would go on.

Nico didn't see his actions as evil. Just doing onto others, what another did onto him. His intention was to infect a large number of women with the HIV virus. He was bitter. And like he said: 'There was no way he was going down alone'.

SIXTEEN

A melancholic Gladys peered from behind proud white net curtains. The image reminded her of that special day. The day this beautiful woman took her son Conteh to be her lawful wedded husband. The day she cried, and blessed them, and sang: "Bind them together, Lord, bind them together. With a cord that can never be broken."

But today she would hold back her tears, tighten her jaws, hold her Bible up to heaven and say: "Lord, forgive the ones who set my son up and put him behind bars." And she would pray for God's forgiveness for Conteh too. For what he had put Simone through. Like she had asked forgiveness for her Sonny for breaking her heart too. But she didn't know if Simone forgave her son, for she was broken it seemed, beyond repair, buy deception and lies.

Gladys opened her front door and hugged Simone. Simone was surprised at her mother-in-law's sobs. Life seemed to have hardened her. Made her tough. She had concluded that older black women found ways of expressing hurt other than tears.

Simone cried too, for it felt like the last farewell. Simone had told her before of her intentions. Gladys didn't expect Simone to be a martyr like she was, giving her all and getting nothing in return. Simone was from a different generation, and when the going gets rough, this new generation gets going, Gladys decided.

Besides, Simone had already forgiven once too often. And Gladys had tried but failed to tell her what she had felt all along. That she wished she had the chance to live her life again. To bring out that fire that lay deep within her. To have emerged from the depression of Sonny's oppression. To have tried to love again. But she had lived on her promise to God. Richer, poorer, better, worst, sickness, health, the stale smell of strange women's perfume — and one too many doses of STD.

Two weeks later, Simone had got used to the *For Sale* sign outside her house. She had to leave the past behind. Bury a dead marriage. And a good way to start was to get rid of the marital home. She had already told Conteh, in a letter, what her plans were, and he agreed. Reluctantly.

Collette was the last to pull up outside the STD clinic. She was reluctant to go in as she would rather not be seen there at all. Joya and Carmen were already there, sitting at a deliberate distance from each other. Carmen was already there when Joya walked in, and it was too late to do a u-turn. Collette walked up to the reception desk and it felt as if all eyes were on her. She could do nothing but wait like the rest of them, in the less than dignified place, reflecting with disdain on who had brought them here — Conteh.

Under different circumstances, the women would have been returning dirty looks. Cutting their eyes and showing contempt for each other. Now they looked only at their own feet. The feeling of each other's presence was enough. It was like the post-feeling of having you skirt,

unknowingly hitched in your knickers, exposing your ass
Or the late discovery of soiled toilet paper on the sole of
your shoe, after a trip to the bog.

There was no need to ask why they were all sitting in
this STD clinic. There were loud shouts from the
grapevine, and their ears were open. Now, all three baby
mothers were here to find out if Conteh had given them
the kiss of death.

It was almost as if Fate had brought them there on the
same day. As if someone ensured that the three ladies'
appointments were on the same day, and within minutes of
each other. It was almost too strange to be a coincidence.

The waiting room was quiet. An attractive woman with
a teenage girl walked in. The teenage girl was pushing a
pushchair, and if Gladys Gonzalez could see the baby in
this pushchair, she would be convinced she was looking at
Conteh, as a baby, all over again. Blood was too close for
comfort. Jacqueline had heard the news too, and had taken
her daughter Cerise and her grandson for an AIDS test.

But she had not told Cerise the full story. She would
take that to her grave.

A host of quiet eyes came to rest on the sweet gurgling
baby boy. It crossed Joya's mind how much the baby
looked like her own when it was first born. He had
Conteh's eyes, nose, dimples and those cute, pouting lips.

Carmen and Collette were thinking the same thing. But
none of them thought that Cerise's baby was their
children's little brother, and Cerise herself, their children's
sister.

Joya, Carmen and Collette left the clinic knowing that it

was too late for them, and a few others, since they had already infected a section of the population of Birmingham with the dreaded virus. Someone should have told the ladies: 'If you lay down with dogs, you will wake up with fleas'.

"Don't you want to see my beautiful body? I'll let you touch it. You can if you want to." The attractive black woman had the old white man and his wife bemused by her persistent need to bare her body.

It was hot. The park was overflowing with people, but she chose him — a frail, yet distinguished looking man with weather-beaten skin and silver hair. He had kind eyes, but they could not help her.

Her startling beauty, her healthy skin, her manicured nails and the way she was dressed told the old man that she was no tramp.

The couple moved to another seat.

The troublesome woman followed.

"All I need is an orgasm. Honest. Please make me come. Make me come, you bastard! Make me come!" She became aggressive.

"What is your name?" A middle aged white woman tried to talk to the pleading beauty, who was now crouched on the grass in front of the patient man, who had nothing for her but a bemused expression.

"Why me?" The old man asked hypothetically.

A crowd now gathered around as if it was a freak show.

The classily dressed woman stood up and attempted to take her clothes off.

"No. You can't do that, miss." The Florence Nightingale tried to stop her. "Does anyone know her?" She turned expectantly to the curious spectators, but was confronted with a few shakes of heads and mostly mocking smiles from injudicious young men. "Did she not have any belongings with her, like a handbag or anything?" She turned to the old man and his wife, the victims of the woman's attention.

"I don't think so." The man spoke with a kind voice.

"I've got breast like plums, you know. They're beautiful. Where are my stilettos? Come on, Fred." The woman reached out to the old man again.

"She thinks I'm Fred now," the old man mumbled to his wife.

"Are you all right, miss?"

An assertive voice broke the easiness of the inquisitive crowd. A female police officer had arrived with a male colleague. She tried to talk to the now half-dressed woman, but she was oblivious to her presence. She danced provocatively, making sexual gestures with her body. A young man laughed a bit too loud and she switched so fast it startled the whole crowd. She lounged at him, knocked him down and damn near ripped his balls off.

"Get her off me," he screamed. "Fuck man, she's gonna kill me!"

The police officers were amazed at the strength of the slim woman. It took both of them and two other men to release the screaming man from her grip. There was no guarantee that his privates would be of any use to him now.

"I'll burn your fucking house down, too, Conteh! I will!" She protested as the officers led her away.

The crowd watched as she was bundled with care into a police car. A dose of sedatives helped the process.

Her name was Marcia. She was taken to a mental hospital, where she would be given the care she needed.

"Are you okay, Marcia?" a friendly black nurse rested her hand on the beautiful woman's right shoulder. Marcia was now rocking back and forth on a chair, the only comfort she knew. She liked the sensation of movement while resting. She didn't know why, she just did. She didn't even know who she was, or why she was sitting in this rocking chair, like a docile pup. She didn't know that there was a place called Sollihul, where she once lived in a luxury flat, and that she still had a healthy bank account, inherited from an old eccentric white man, called Fred, who she once gave the opportunity to gaze upon her beautiful ebony body.

She was oblivious to everything, so she didn't know why she found the need (and summoned strength) to snarl at every black male that happen to walk by. She didn't know that she had fallen in love with a handsome bastard called Conteh Gonzalez, who couldn't give her what she wanted in the end — real love and commitment. So how could she remember that she had torched his Beema and watched it go up in flames?

And AIDS? Who would tell her? How would they tell her.

"A'right, Marcia?" She didn't even recognise her own

name, let alone this woman's voice — the woman with sorrow-filled eyes that was now combing her hair. Marcia recognised a slight familiarity though; a familiarity of comfort that generated from this woman's breast. She stopped rocking and lay there. Still.

The tears from her mother's eyes fell upon Marcia's hair. And she brushed it. And combed. And patted. And even though she feared that Marcia was oblivious to what she was saying, she spoke, her Jamaican accent strong, penetrating and telling.

"He took yuh sanity, chile. Took yuh heart an' finally yuh mind. You were doing so well. Until yuh met him. Conteh Gonzalez has so much to answer for."

SEVENTEEN

"I, Simone Marian King... Take you, Lawrence Lloyd Hendricks... To be my husband. To have and to hold from this day forward. For better for worse. For richer for poorer. In sickness and in health. To love and to cherish. Till death us do part. According to God's holy law. This is my solemn vow."

Simone couldn't help reflecting on the first time she had made those vows. She had meant them, too. But, 'If your left eye affect you, pluck it out'. She had quoted that to Gladys when she told her of her decision to end the marriage to her son. Gladys could not disagree with a quote from the Bible.

Lawrence looked deep into her eyes with a promise of foreverness. His whole body shook as he held her soft fingers in his hands.

The aura of their happiness was contagious.

Janet looked at Sandra and they both smiled at each other with tear-filled eyes. For them, the moment was both happy and sad. Sad that they had lost Simone as their true sister-in-law, but happy that, as far as they could see, she had found happiness after all. They knew she was in love, _really_ in love, with Lawrence, and wished her all the best.

From the back row of this peaceful church, filled with well-wishers for the happy couple, Gladys wiped a tear from her eye. It felt as if she had lost her own daughter.

From the back of Simone's flowing dress, her veil, and the sound of her voice saying 'I do," she couldn't help remembering her son's own wedding to the same bride. Now he was sitting in a prison cell. She asked the Lord, "Why?"

"If there is anyone, knowing of any impediments or any reason why these two should not be joined together in holy matrimony, let him speak now, or forever hold his peace."

The Vicar cast his eyes over the congregation as usual, expecting nothing. But he was shocked when a response came from the back. The whole church turned in horror. Nico was stood there, looking worse for wear, shouting, "He loved you, Simone! He *loved* you! He still does, man! Today is killing him! You are killing him!"

Nico had had one too many. Two sturdy men ejected him before he could spoil such a beautiful day.

"You are now man and wife together."

The whole church cheered. Lawrence took the 'you may now kiss the bride' to some extreme. His lips seemed to be glued to her lips, causing the congregation to cheer again.

Simone smiled at everyone as she walked back down the isle with her new husband. She stopped with purpose, and held Gladys' hand and squeezed hard. "You will always be 'mum' to me. Nothing has changed there."

Gladys dried her eyes and caught another pair of friendly eyes. She returned a smile as she did years before, when Simone had married her son. A smile from Simone's mum. She had flown in from Jamaica to share in her daughter's happiness for the second time. And the smiles both mothers returned said: 'Let's hope it works this time.'

"Mrs Captain Lawrence Hendricks, eh? So dreams do come true after all," Lawrence whispered in Simone's ear as a shower of confetti sealed their happiness.

A faithful pair of hands guided the trailing veil into the waiting limousine. Simone looked at her best mate and smiled. Pam confessed and apologised to her for unintentionally sleeping with Conteh. Her sunken eyes and sallow skin would not have stopped her from being there for her friend. It was what she had always wanted for her — happiness. And she hoped it would last, forever.

The happy couple honeymooned in Paris, making heavenly love, relaxing in each other's arms, drinking wine, feeling fine, and getting to know more about each other. Only six months prior, Simone sat in Lawrence's luxury home, listening to him breaking off a sexual relationship that he had already told her about. She admired his open honesty and hoped she wasn't dreaming.

"Are you sure you're happy?" Lawrence asked Simone on the last day of their honeymoon.

"If I wasn't, then my name wouldn't be Simone Marian Hendricks." It sounded good, and Simone repeated it over and over again. It sounded good to Lawrence too. He pulled her close and kissed her, remembering the song they had danced to on their wedding day. 'It'll take an eternity to break us.'

He was sure he had found heaven.

On the flight home, Simone thought of how grateful she was to whoever invented femidoms, the protection she

used without Conteh even being aware, and confirmed
that skin to skin is all in the mind.

Once your man has an affair, you can never fully trust
him again. Simone hadn't trusted Conteh for years, ever
since his very first affair. He had only admitted to it when
she caught him red-handed. There was nothing to stop him
having affairs until he was caught again. Until then, she
had decided to use protection. She took control of
everything, and Conteh fell hook, line and sinker for her
sudden dislike for that good old cunnilingus.

She felt lucky, and knew just how much when she
looked at the man that sat next to her on the BA jet.

"Nearer my God to thee, nearer to thee."

Gladys couldn't get to church today, so the church had
come to her. Soaring blood pressure was giving her a run
for her faith. Handbags laden with Bibles decorated the
floor of her front room. The singing and praying had
ended and the church sisters chatted away like over-sized
teenagers at recess.

Conversations swung to and fro like topsy-turvy wind:
"So Brother Johnson pas' away?" asked one sister. "Yes.
Gone to meet his maker," said another. "An' Sista Morgan
tek a tu'n feh de worse." Short kissing of teeth expressed
remorse rather than disgust. "The Lord givet' an' He taket'
away," sealed a conversation in one corner of the room.

"Janet," Gladys turned to her daughter beside her. "Go
slice up some pitayta puddin' feh de bredrin, dear." Even
in her illness, she aimed to please.

It had been over a week since Janet had been staying

with her mum. She had booked leave when she detected a dreaded 'finality' in her mother's conversation. Gladys talked wills, deeds, insurance policies, contents and living righteous.

"Mum, stop talking like this," her children would say in turn, for Gladys looked a bill of health.

"I feel it so I know it," she would reply.

He had served three years of his sentence, but Conteh still hadn't got used to prison life and was still trying to get another appeal going. But with no wife who believed in him to work for him on the outside, things had slowed down and the possibility that he might be inside for the duration was beginning to dawn on him. As Conteh walked down to the visiting room, the last chapter he had just read from his Bible, rang in his head. Isaiah 55, verse 9. *"Jesus wept."* It was the shortest verse in the Bible, and one that would stay in his mind for a while. It would stop him feeling so less manly for letting his tears flow today, his birthday. 'If Jesus could cry,' he had thought, 'who am I to think crying is a soft thing to do?'

Janet and Sandra were sitting at a table in a far corner of the visiting room. Pastor Brown stood like the Pope, holding his Bible.

"Where's mum?" was the first thing he said, even before he sat down. The girls looked at each other, wondering which one of them would take the job of telling him.

Pastor Brown reached for Conteh's hand and held it.

"Conteh, mum's had a stroke. She's in the hospital."

Janet said. "It's not critical. She'll live. But we don't yet know how much brain damage she's suffered."

"She's in the hands of God, Conteh. He will take care of her." Pastor did what he did best.

"Then why did He let this happen to her then? Why? I'm the one who deserves a fucking stroke!"

Pastor Brown didn't seem bothered by the swearing.

"Too much stress and worry can bring on a stroke you know, Conteh." Sandra showed her presence. "Mum had been through a lot. Your situation now for instance. All that pent-up stress had to come out somewhere, you know."

Sandra was always straight. It was never in her nature to beat around the bush. If she felt it, she would say it, and now she didn't see the point in hitting her brother with a soft cushion.

"Okay, sis. I'm already feeling bad enough. I know I helped to bring this stroke on. I know she's a worrier. I just wish I could turn the clock back."

"Stop blaming yourself, bro'." Janet tried to make it easy on him.

Conteh reflected on the root of his downfall — that tempting bit of flesh that lay hidden at the meeting of a woman's thigh. So simple, yet great enough to bring down an empire.

"Why didn't I listen to her, sis?"

"Listen to who?" Janet asked.

"Mum." Conteh fiddled with the edge of the settee.

"None of us did, bro'. Except for Sandra of course. Even when she ripped the skins off our behinds for sneaking out to lose ourselves in what she called 'devil music'." She chuckled. "We couldn't see the danger in scrambling down drainpipes could we? I suppose the world would have been too perfect if we had listened."

"Feh real."

"Her dream was right, pastor. I'm in a cage and my wings are well and truly clipped.

"Let's have a word of prayer." Pastor Brown readied himself.

Janet dragged the last of her cigarette. Before she bowed her head, she looked around the room. Everyone was looking over at the sanctified table. Their attentions were attracted when Pastor Brown commenced, in a forceful voice: "Father God, we call upon thy mercy..."

The praying was over and the conversation had calmed.

"Anyway, happy birthday," Janet wished she could slip her brother a birthday spliff.

Sandra simply sighed. She was not comfortable with the place. However rude her brother was, she knew he shouldn't be there.

All too soon a bell rang and bodies rose reluctantly all over the room. Visiting time was over for everyone.

"We're all praying hard," Conteh. "It will be okay."

Conteh wished he could believe the pastor's latter words. From his side of the fence it seemed highly unlikely.

The little Pentecostal church seemed almost unreal to Conteh. He was sat between two prison officers and felt like a property of Her Majesty. They were there to ensure that he returned to the inner walls of Her Majesty's prison, safely. He was here for one reason. To mourn the death of his dear mother. Gladys's condition had deteriorated rapidly over the past six weeks, right up to her demise.

Conteh sat, looking back over his life. He had cried so much over the past few weeks, and now it seemed he couldn't cry at all. He was numb. Almost hardened.

The open coffin stood there like a morbid showpiece, exhibiting his deceased mother. Tears were flowing every which way, as people queued up to pay their last respects to the peaceful corpse. The organist played, 'Lord, I'm coming home,' and it was a task to find a dry eye in the church.

Sandra stared at her mother's face, her crossed hands, her well-dressed body, lying there as if she was sleeping. She wanted to shake her mother. Wake her up. Couldn't she see her children needed her?

"Sandra?"

A church sister was ensuring that Sandra hadn't fallen into a trance. Sandra didn't look up. Instead she lay her palm across her mother's crossed hands, and kissed her cold forehead. As she lifted her head, a tear fell upon her mother's left cheek. She left it there.

Janet sat in a trance, eyes fixed on the casket. She hadn't cried since her mother died.

A mournful voice echoed:

Sleep on beloved, sleep and take thy rest

It was a cue for the heart-jerking hymn, and the whole congregation followed:

Lay down thy head upon thy Saviour's breast

There were tear-filled hankies everywhere.

We love thee well, but Jesus loves thee best

Sister Vennah howled like a distressed wolf. She was hanging over the coffin, arms outspread.

Good night, good night, good night...

The words twisted the knife of sorrow that was already lodged in Sandra's heart, and her wailing became uncontrollable. She was led away towards the vestry, her eyes fixed on her mother's casket. It was poignant. Like the silent panning away of a camera from a sad scene in a heart-wrenching movie.

Conteh didn't join the queue for a last glimpse at his mother. He wanted to remember her smiling face. Her haughty Jamaican laugh filled with sunshine and kindness. He didn't want to see her solemn, lifeless composure. And he would not go to the burial ground either. He was hurting, but like Janet he couldn't cry.

He saw Simone and had to say something. She came over to where he was sitting between the two burly prison officers, his eyes filled with sorrow.

Conteh squeezed his ex-wife's fingers and smiled. He clearly still loved her.

"I've messed up big time haven't I? She told me I'd lose you one day. I should have listened to her. She loved you, Simone," he said. "To the max. But you knew that didn't you, babes?" He paused. "If only I could turn the clock back, Simone. I'm sorry. I know it won't change anything but, believe me, I am. I was a fool. If it's any consolation, I'm suffering for it now. Mum always used to say, 'a cow never know the use of its tail until he loses it.' She was so right."

"It's all in the past, Conteh. I've got over it. I'm happy now."

Just then, it all got too much for her. She had to leave the church. She would always pay respects to Gladys.

Lawrence was waiting for her at home. She squeezed her Conteh's hand and said nothing. She hated goodbyes.

"There you are," said Lawrence when Simone walked through the door.

"Something smells nice."

"Thought you'd like Chinese," he said, holding her close and kissing her gently.

But food was the last thing on her mind. She wanted to be loved. Held. Comforted. As she responded to his affection, she couldn't but smile again at the picture that met her eyes — the one that made her wonder if the same photographer worked the whole of the West Indies with his little black and white camera. A warm picture of Lawrence at eight years old and his sister only six. His attractive mother and handsome father stood proud behind them, in a garden in Antigua. A wonderful life, Lawrence had told her, his parents had lived together. As far as he knew, his father had kept his vows, forsaking all others and clinging only to his mother.

"Aren't you hungry?" Lawrence asked, after a long passionate kiss. He avoided the topic of funerals.

"Yes. For you," said Simone, holding her husband's hand and climbing the stairs to their bedroom. Today it would be special. She would delight in watching his expression — an expression that would contrast that of Conteh's. The joy in his eyes. The thankfulness in his voice.

The love that would generate even more, when she tells him that his wish had come true. The wish for a love child.

The drive back to jail was sad and lonely. Sad when he remembered his mother, lonely when he remembered the wife he once had, and wondered why women always seemed to look better once they left him. Simone looked 'boom' in black. He swallowed hard and tried to tell himself that life goes on. The car made its way slowly down Soho Road, where Conteh had once cruised like a lone ranger. Sitting their in handcuffs, he reminisced and swallowed hard. He didn't want to leave the area. Figured he knew just how a Mandinkan felt, being dragged out of Africa. He hadn't realised how much he was attached to the place. Outside Scratcher's Yard, where he had won his first dancehall trophy and where he had rubbed the skirts off many a gal, he saw a faded tatty poster for Vibes Injection. The tears started streaming down his face now.

Conteh closed his eyes as if to shut the whole world out. He fell into a trance-like slumber.

"Bwoy yuh live by pussy, yuh die by pussy!" The guard he was handcuffed to mocked with disdain. For a white guy he had mastered the Jamaican lingo to a T. He must have repeated the taunt no less than a dozen times and Conteh was ready to commit murder. *Feh real.*

"Come on, Gonzalez, yuh lickle raasclaat! Wake up!"

Conteh opened his eyes.

The car was pulling into the prison gate.

END